Roberta Latow has be[...] Springfield, Massachusetts and New York City. She has also been an international interior designer in the USA, Europe, Africa and the Middle East, travelling extensively to acquire arts, artefacts and handicrafts. Her sense of adventure and her experiences on her travels have enriched her writing; her fascination with heroic men and women; how and why they create the lives they do for themselves; the romantic and erotic core within – all these themes are endlessly interesting to her, and form the subjects and backgrounds of her novels.

Praise for Roberta Latow's previous novels:

'Passion on a super-Richter scale . . . Roberta Latow's unique brand of erotic writing remains fresh and exciting' *Daily Telegraph*

'A wonderful storyteller. Her descriptive style is second to none . . . astonishing sexual encounters . . . exotic places, so real you can almost feel the hot sun on your back . . . heroines we all wish we could be . . . irresistible' Jane Green, *Express*

'Latow's writing is vibrant and vital. Her descriptions emanate a confidence and boldness that is typical of her characters . . . you can't help but be swept along by them. A pleasure to read' *Books* magazine

Body and Soul

Roberta Latow

HEADLINE

First published in 2001
by HEADLINE BOOK PUBLISHING

First published in paperback in 2001
by HEADLINE BOOK PUBLISHING

10 9 8 7 6 5 4 3 2 1

ISBN 0 7472 5959 3

Typeset by Avon Dataset Ltd, Bidford-on-Avon, Warks

Printed and bound in Great Britain by
Mackays of Chatham plc, Chatham, Kent

HEADLINE BOOK PUBLISHING
A division of Hodder Headline
338 Euston Road
London NW1 3BH

www.headline.co.uk
www.hodderheadline.com

For Michael Booth and Stephen Thorpe,
friends who add to one's life

I gave in completely
my body, my soul

Chapter 1

Edna Archer and Beryl Pike, having shrugged out of their clear plastic raincoats and then their puffy navy blue nylon jackets, removed the waterproof scarves from their heads. Shopping carts carefully placed so as not to trip anyone were standing sentinel next to their chairs. The two women were halfway through the Frog's Hollow tea room Thursday special: roast pork, stewed apple, roast potatoes and parsnips, balls of Paxo stuffing, Brussels sprouts and pools of Bisto gravy.

It was their Thursday ritual: the week's shopping, lunch out at Frog's Hollow, a brief exchange with the regulars. The highlight of lunch apart from the price – £2.75 for old age pensioners, £3.25 for everyone else – was always Eden Sidd. Just seeing her was uplifting for them. She was their very own celebrity. Though they were aware that she was a famous cellist, they had never heard her play except once on TV and then only because Beryl, changing channels, had caught the performance by mistake and immediately called Edna to switch on her set.

1

After seeing the performance the two women agreed Eden Sidd and her music were beyond them but that had no bearing on their liking for her and enjoyment of their Thursday chats with her: the butcher's lamb's liver, the bakery's special price on baps if bought in lots of two dozen or more, too many people waiting in line at the Co-op till, the WI stall being sold out of cakes by ten o'clock.

They knew her Thursday schedule almost as well as their own: the hairdresser, the cheese shop, a visit to the butcher on the corner (the one they didn't use, too expensive), then lunch at Frog's Hollow before she got into her soft-top black BMW and went home.

Eden Sidd enjoyed her once a week forays into the Gloucestershire town and lunch among the locals, especially Edna and Beryl. It was a world that was alien from the one in which she normally lived. Frog's Hollow, Edna and Beryl, were for Eden a comfort zone, a pleasant and totally uncomplicated slice of normal day-to-day living. For her Thursdays were pure self-indulgence, a taste of the norm, the simple life. Often she would sit talking across the tables to the two women and at the same time marvel at the way discussing the price of a collar of ham with two old dears could be such a luxury in one's life. But it was and she was grateful to have these two confidantes. She often thought as she ate her meal: From Fortnum & Mason to Frog's Hollow – quite a distance. She never could work out whether she had come up in the world or down. She only knew that at this moment in time it didn't matter. Fortnum's or Frog's Hollow – to Eden it made no difference.

Today she entered the tea room rather later than usual. The place was deserted. She was sorry to have missed Edna and Beryl and their shopping carts. They had already been and gone, the cook-owner told her as she came forward and took Eden's order. The two women sat chatting together for a few minutes about who had been in and then the proprietor disappeared into the kitchen.

Eden was well into her meal and enjoying the solitude of dining alone in the tea room when the bell above the door rang and it burst open. A man entered, a gust of wind and a heavy shower of rain blowing in after him.

Eden looked up from her plate. In all the years she had been coming to Frog's Hollow she had never seen him before. He was a man in his mid-thirties, it appeared, impressively handsome, tanned and with a shock of black hair worn on the long side. He was wearing a belted black cashmere coat, the collar turned up against the February elements. He was standing next to Eden but failed to register her. It was as if she was invisible. He opened his coat and shook the rain from it and then, without a glance in her direction, passed by her, his coat grazing her arm.

Eden was devastated. For the first time in her life she had been overlooked as a sexually appealing woman on even the most superficial basis; not so much as a glance, a sideways look, a moment's appreciation of her as an interesting sensuous lady, had he given her. Stunned and upset by the realisation that she had become one of

3

those millions of women who at a certain age become invisible to attractive men on the hunt for sexual liaisons, the scent of death engulfed her.

She remained seated while trying to regain her composure. Eden could hardly take her eyes off the stranger now seated across the empty tables from her. Still he failed to notice her. No longer hungry but determined to finish her meal and put her emotions in order, she waited in the hope that he might finally acknowledge her with a glance. Just a brief look in her direction would be enough to restore her visibility, give her the sense of being alive again as a passionate female soul, one who could still interest a stranger.

For a moment she thought she was rewarded because he did look her way. But she was not. He looked right through her, making her invisibility and the pain it caused her even more acute. She felt dizzy with despair but, much as she wanted to run away from the tea room and her gloomy realisation, unable to move. She watched him finish his plate of lasagne and chips, drink a cup of coffee. Eden waited him out over a pudding of apple crumble and clotted cream. One glance at her on his way out – that was all the hope left to her now.

The stranger paid his bill and shrugged into his coat, turned the collar up and left the tea room still without giving her the glance of recognition she so needed. To add insult to injury, she was even forced to rise from her chair and close the door behind him for in the wake of his departure the wind blew it open and rain rushed in on her.

All the way home she tried to put the incident out of her mind. Tried to rationalise her feelings: tell herself she was over-reacting. How pathetic to have needed sexual attention from a stranger so as to be made to feel erotically appealing and desirable. It didn't work. She felt massively rejected on the most intimate level for a woman. She had seen incidents similar to the one she had just experienced happen to other women, to friends. Was it vanity or wishful thinking that had made her think it could never happen to her?

Eden had always been an outsider, an individual who had known she walked a lonely but bright and interesting road, and had never minded that. Suddenly to find that she was nothing special, merely another of the millions of women her age that society no longer regarded as sensuous and desirable beings but mere shells of those things, was a rude awakening.

Driving through the village and the open gates to the drive of her house she was shocked to find that tears would not stop streaming from her eyes. Eden halted at the front door. The rain still poured down seemingly in sheets and the grey of the sky was as heavy as her heart. The trees, dripping copiously, appeared to have been beaten into a submission of sorts by the weather.

The house was dark and sombre-looking. The faint sound of dogs barking reached her in the car. It snapped her out of that dark place she had slipped into. Opening the car door, she readied herself and then made a dash on to the terrace and through the never-locked front door. She shook the rain from her coat and whipped off her wide-brimmed rain hat, dropping it into a basket where umbrellas, paper parasols and walking sticks lived. A Russian wolfhound, Chekov, and two Shi Tsus, Winkie and Wonkie, vied for her attention with leaps and jumps, barks and dog kisses.

The menagerie followed her through the hall and dining room and into the kitchen where she hung her raincoat on the clothes rack and slipped out of her wet shoes, placing them neatly near the Aga to dry. Eden lifted one of the two copper lids and slid the kettle on to the hot plate before sitting down. Winkie and Wonkie leapt into her lap in a flurry of long silky blonde and white hair, while large and elegant Chekov collapsed lovingly at her feet.

Eden's home was a Queen Anne house of many windows with elegant high-ceilinged rooms on the ground floor. Though it may have appeared sombre on approaching it that rainy day, once inside it was a house of quiet, uplifting simplicity, not at all dark or dreary. Eden loved her home and the life she had been living in it for the past ten years. Though she was not reclusive she had settled for privacy, a quiet life that left behind the strains and stresses of a busy cosmopolitan existence. She had been tired, believed the time had come to retreat and enjoy the fruits of her labours, indulge in a more simple existence. Here she could garden, cook, write music and play the cello for her own enjoyment.

The kettle whistled and she rose from the wing chair at the end of the long wooden table and made herself a pot of tea. She was feeling more comfortable about the silly incident in the tea room. For a few minutes she actually thought she had shaken off that uncomfortable feeling of having become something less even than the shell of an attractive woman. Of being dead to all she had been as a sexual being, of having become an old woman, one she didn't recognise or know. After tea she went to the music room and lit a fire, took up her cello and played for two hours. Music was her life. It had always been that way and even now in her retirement she practised at least five hours a day.

Over dinner, an omelette, salad and a glass of wine consumed by the open fire in the kitchen, Eden realised that she had not after all accepted the incident in the tea room with good grace. She did not want to be sexually insignificant to a stranger or, more to the point, to herself. That evening in bed the one thought in her mind was that she was no longer the woman she'd thought she was. Half the night she was haunted by questions. Where had all the love, sex and passion gone? When and why had she cut them out of her heart, her very being? Eden began to wonder if they had ever really been there. Time, the mind and loneliness can play tricks with reality, and more than any of those things loss can distort the truth as memory struggles to conjure up what once was but has long since vanished.

Eden was haunted by a realisation of what she had lost. The love affairs and sexual encounters that had been so much a part of her life – they had happened, hadn't they?

There was no sleep for her that night. She rose from

her bed and paced the room in the dark. The rain was gone, the clouds had been blown away and the dark sky was filled with stars. A crescent moon lit her bedroom and the garden rolling down to the wood and the lake.

In the morning the housekeeper arrived and Eden was momentarily distracted from her anguish by the need to give instructions to Rachel. It never ceased to amaze her how much work there was to running a house and garden, a few dogs and a car, even on such a modest scale as this. She pondered on that as she went over the chores with Rachel but somehow could not keep focused on the list. Her mind wandered to other things: how much more time it took to keep her health and looks together nowadays, the interminable red tape that had to be waded through just to keep things ticking over. Hers was now a life mundane beyond any she could ever have imagined for herself in the past. It frightened her, but not so much as it shocked her.

Rachel Morgan was a good housekeeper, a local woman in her mid-thirties, married with two daughters. She was devoted to Eden, had learned how to run the house the way Eden liked to live in it and was at times dazzled by how famous her employer's friends were. Rachel was curious about the men who on occasion, and for short periods of time, became a part of Eden's life. At times she'd felt anxious that one of them might enter it for good and change Eden's way of life.

When Rachel had first started work, Eden used to travel considerably more than she had been doing for the last few years. Greece, Turkey, Egypt, Fiji, Hong

Kong, India ... A brief announcement that she was visiting friends and off she would go. They were intimate friends as housekeeper and employer but worlds apart in every other way. Rachel was happy working for Eden but at the same time jealous and possessive of her, and Eden Sidd was not a woman to be controlled.

She was aware of that flaw in their relationship but was not certain if her housekeeper was. But then there was something in Eden's character that made some of her friends as well as her housekeeper feel that she needed to be controlled by them. There was about her an air of vulnerability, an innocence that was at odds with the sophisticated woman she was, the hugely creative and professional person of enormous passion and sensitivity. She was known for her wit and charm and for being clever, a caring person. She had her flaws and one of her greatest was that she was too soft, over-sensitive. She could be crushed by the hardness of others. How many times in her life had she heard people ask her, 'Why do you care?' It was a question she never seemed able to answer.

After her meeting with Rachel, Eden talked to the gardener but was unable to be constructive or creative about what she wanted done in the garden, resistant to his suggestions about thinning out the wood, so called the meeting to an abrupt end. The postman arrived and there were too many letters to deal with. She could concentrate on nothing. Her mind kept slipping back to happier times, the past and what her life had once been like, in spite of the fact that she had been very happy these last ten years in her country retirement. A feeling came over her then: a pressing need to affirm in some way that the excitement of the erotic life and loves she had once enjoyed had been real, as much fun as she remembered it to have been.

In late morning a girl friend, Anna Bascomb, called.

'I can hear in your voice you're not having a happy day. It always gives you away. Do you want to tell me about it?'

'Not particularly.'

'Come down to London, it's ages since you were here. We'll do the art exhibitions if you like. Lunch somewhere that's amusing and terribly expensive if it's on you, somewhere more modest if it's on me. Do the windows on Bond Street, and you can get Charlie Chan to cut your hair. It's months since you've done that.'

'You are incorrigible and I am not going down to London. I'm filled with dread at the prospect and it would do nothing to calm me down.'

'What would then?' asked Anna.

'I don't know. I haven't worked it out yet.'

Anna and Eden had been close friends for more than twenty years and knew and understood each other very well. Or so each of them thought. Anna had once been the wife of George Chen, conductor of the Boston Symphony Orchestra. She was a *femme fatale* who'd seduced George away from a wife and five children, married him, and after two years split up from him. She chose to move on to someone who was not married to music and could give her the attention she demanded;

he settled down with a young pianist who demanded nothing but to sit in awe at his feet. Anna and her present husband, Warrington Bascomb, lived in total adoration of each other. Her special charm was a *joie de vivre* that captivated husbands, lovers and her many girl friends.

It did not take long before she managed to find out what was bothering Eden. There was a momentary pause then that seemed endless to Eden before Anna took up the conversation again.

'How rotten for you, Eden. I can remember how I felt the first time it happened to me.'

'You never said anything?'

'No. I'm not as strong as you are. I was so devastated that I went for help to get over it. You see, I don't have the inner resources you have. Men had always been my life. Being attractive, having them want me, was all I had. To know that I could pull them and keep them, gain the love and stability I craved, was everything to me once. My encounter happened at a taxi rank at the Grosvenor House. That ride home of a mere few streets was soul-destroying. It happened when I was between husbands. I wept like a child then pulled myself together and went for several sessions with a Jungian therapist. It took some doing to get my self-esteem back on track. Aren't men bastards? What are you going to do?'

'This has been a jolt. More than anything I keep thinking how much fun sex was once, how I miss the excitement of youth and romance and love affairs. That there's nothing in this world to replace that. Why did I let it all go? How could I have succumbed to the social

11

politics that brainwash mature women into believing they're redundant as sensual, sexual beings? Must give up erotic experience because age has settled upon them. That youth has a monopoly on sexuality where men are concerned. How did I fall into the loveless trap? What made me stop demanding an exciting sex life? Because I didn't think it was seemly to indulge in great sex as I grew old? What pathetic foolishness to give up pleasure so as not to look desperate in the eyes of my peers.

'What am I going to do? you ask. I don't know exactly. But I can tell you what I am *not* going to do and that is to lie down and die, vanish into self-induced spinster-hood! I'll have to find a way to go out into the world and validate who I have been, who and what I am at present. I'm going to shrug off this middle-aged thinking, try to find another way to regain the fun I once had in my youth. A therapist might have been best for you but I believe I'm able to re-evaluate my past unaided and create a new present for myself as rich and varied as the happiest of sexual times I ever had in the past.'

The women spoke for another ten minutes and by the time they'd finished their conversation it was clear to Anna that Eden was at a crossroads in her life. She feared for her then because older women among Anna's friends had rarely been able to recapture their once erotic life styles and make them work for them in their mature years, as she had done. Some had been too obviously trying to recapture their youth; others, having gone about it in a more subtle manner, for the most part fared no better. Eden? Anna wondered about her and what she might do, how she might find sexual fulfilment and love again. She had, after all, had it several times in her life already.

Chapter 2

Eden wondered how she could have looked and not seen the void in her otherwise happy existence. Or was it a chasm rather than a void? One she had been jumping over, back and forth, with such ease she had had not the least idea that it was there: something fundamental missing from her life.

The days passed and then it was Thursday and she was back in Frog's Hollow having lunch across the room from Edna and Beryl. The tea room was filled with the Thursday regulars, the conversation with the two women was much as it always was, but Eden found that, for the first time, she was having to make an effort whereas before that fateful Thursday being cordial and interested in them had come so easily, had felt so genuine.

The fun of belonging even for an hour in their world was gone. Had she just been playing a game with herself and these good people, fooling them all into thinking she belonged in a simple world like this? The food in her mouth turned to ashes and yet it was the same Thursday fare she had enjoyed these past ten years. The stranger did not reappear. That afternoon Eden went home and took a nap. On waking she dozed for several minutes and her mind slipped back in time.

She was young, beautiful, talented. Music was her life above and beyond anything else. Her father was first violinist with the Boston Symphony Orchestra; her mother, Leila Sidd, an accomplished pianist.

Leila was a great beauty who loved fast cars and exciting men. A woman of seductive charm on a grand scale, she was vain and luxury-loving, passionate, interested in herself first, her daughter second, and her husband third, if somewhat marginally. She was a well-known figure in the upper echelons of the international classical music world. The sort of woman for whom men bought houses in the South of France, Paris couture clothes and jewels. All the things that she could easily have afforded to buy for herself, in fact, as a Boston heiress of considerable wealth.

The Sidds were much gossiped about: chiefly Leila's publicly conducted love affairs with famous men and the fact that she, her husband and daughter remained a family in spite of their hardly ever living together under the same roof longer than several weeks in a year. The three of them were devoted to each other, in their fashion, and shared a special unconventional love that was rare in their circle. Leila and Teddy Sidd were great travellers, he for his work, Leila for fun, and they took their daughter with them whenever possible.

They loved Eden for her beauty, sweetness, and above

all because she shared their passion for music. She was extraordinarily talented and they gave her everything a gifted child needed to make something of herself. Whatever she learned about love was through these two extraordinary parents and her mother's and father's lovers, amorous friends, who were an acknowledged part of Eden's life.

In their own outlandishly liberal way both Teddy and Leila were protective of their daughter. They were careful not to allow her to slip into the pigeon-hole labelled 'child prodigy', having seen too many young talents slide into that role and never progress from it into world-class, timeless success.

It was Leila who, by example and affection for her daughter, taught Eden to enjoy her beauty and femininity, instilled in her a passion for the sexual liaisons that enhance a certain type of woman's life. Her mother kept Eden dressed in provocative, attractive clothes to flatter her stunning figure, sensuous face and long dark hair. Leila wanted her daughter to be admired as she herself had been by men. She wanted Eden to enjoy her own good looks as well as her talent so that she might have a full and rounded life.

Eden was one of those rare creatures blessed with it all. She knew as much from a young age, having been born that way. All who met and became involved with her, in even the most superficial manner, were instantly aware of it too.

In a half dreaming state, Eden smiled to herself as memories of that time so long ago came to mind. They were followed by a vivid picture of her first love, Marshall Greenspan. She was seventeen, he twenty-nine, handsome as a Greek god, fiercely intelligent with a commanding voice. He was an architect with a passion for music, an authority on the architecture of the great opera houses of the world. Marshall was New York Jewish intelligentsia, the handsome darling of the cognoscenti who dictated the tune to which the arts world, so richly patronised in that city, danced. He had a reputation as a lover of women of all ages and types, in and out of his particular milieu.

Marshall was giving a lecture on opera houses at the Juilliard School of Music when he first saw Eden in the audience of fresh young students he enjoyed teaching. She stood out from the entire sea of faces he was addressing. Her beauty was the first attraction for him but then, as his eyes searched her out time and again during his lecture, he knew that it was more than that. Her sexuality was enticing. He was, even while still standing at the lectern, obsessed by sexual desire for her. She had what he liked most in young women: an obvious sensuality coupled with an air of inexperience.

As for Eden, she was besotted by his good looks, his charismatic command over his audience, passion for his subject and ability to reach into her heart, her very soul. There was something raunchy in the manner in which he looked at her. It made her squirm with sexual desire. He was the first man she had ever seen who made her want him. This was the man to whom she wanted to give up her virginity. He wrapped his sexuality around her. Without even touching her, never even directly addressing her, he induced in her a fiery lust. She came as she sat watching and listening to him, and entered into a state of utter bewilderment and fear.

Nothing like that had ever happened to Eden before. There had been boyfriends and petting and kissing but she had never felt what she felt that afternoon for Marshall Greenspan. Her heart raced with fear of such powerful feelings that were not aroused by music. Here it was, the erotic soul of Eden Sidd, born and in full blossom in almost the same instant – and she with not the least idea what to do about it.

As applause from the students filled her ears and people rose from their chairs to leave she watched a bevy of girls and boys rush to the dais to talk to Marshall. He seemed even more charismatic to her now. Her knees felt weak and unsteady but she did manage to rise from her chair. Had she imagined that he had singled her out, found her attractive?

It was winter and she was slipping into her fox-lined poplin raincoat when she was rewarded with an answer to that particular question. Eden caught Marshall looking at her over the students' heads and across the sea of empty chairs around her. This time he smiled at her. She smiled back, her heart raced, and she gathered all the composure she could summon to leave the auditorium without a backward glance.

The Sidds maintained a New York penthouse apartment on Park Avenue. It had been in Leila's family since the building had been erected in the early 1900s. Eden was grateful that both Leila and Teddy were there with her just then. She knew she could go to either one of her parents and tell them she had fallen hopelessly in love with Marshall Greenspan. That somehow made her feel relaxed and happy and in some sort of dream world where she had never been before.

Standing in front of the school with her cello on the pavement next to her, Eden was trying in vain to hail a cab to take her home while her head was occupied with trying to hold on to the memory of Marshall Greenspan's smile. It had been for her and only her, she was certain of that. Eden was flattered, intrigued by his attention. Her sexual desire for him had not abated. She wanted to hold on to that as well as his smile. She felt a desperate need once again to experience the sensation of orgasm she had felt in the midst of all her fellow students during Marshall Greenspan's seduction of her.

'Hello,' was all he said when he came up behind her.

Even his voice was sexy. It commanded her heart. She turned to look at him. 'I'm having trouble finding a cab.'

He gave a shrill whistle and a cab pulled up sharply in front of them. 'I'm famished – going to Hamburger Heaven. Why don't you come along with me?' he asked as he entered the cab with her cello and then extended a hand to her.

Eden was amazed but silently slipped on to the seat next to him. Rather than let her hand go he brought it to his lips and kissed her fingers. She was actually trembling with excitement as he leaned forward and placed his lips upon hers, kissing her with a tenderness as searing as a hot flame.

Still holding her hand, he gave the taxi driver their destination and then, turning back to Eden, untied the belt around her waist and unbuttoned her coat. Opening it the better to look at her, he told her, 'I find you utterly beautiful, very sexy,' and caressed her face with his hands.

Eden closed her eyes and melted under his touch. She had no defences against such a sweet and exciting seduction, and more to the point she didn't want any. She was aware that he knew that and in some strange way it gave her a certain power over him she didn't even bother to analyse. She merely enjoyed being where she was. They both realised that she would deny him nothing. Every fibre in her body was calling out 'take me'.

They did have their hamburgers at Hamburger Heaven and it was there that he first learned her name. Marshall, of course, knew both her mother and father though not intimately. He was a part of their world and it delighted him that this young woman whom his libido demanded he must conquer was their issue.

'Will you come to dinner with me tomorrow night? Afterwards I'll take you to meet some friends at a party,' he suggested as the doorman on patrol in front of her building opened the cab door.

Marshall carefully handed the cello to him then turned back to face Eden. He could see the sexual longing for him in her eyes. She remained seated, wanting to go home with Marshall Greenspan, for him

21

to ravage her with his lust. The doorman retreated into the lobby of the apartment building. People were rushing past on the pavement, on their way home or to some smart lounge or bar for the customary end-of-the-day Martini to set them up for a social evening.

Marshall pulled Eden gently towards him. With one arm around her waist, he passionately kissed her lips as he slipped his hand under her skirt and between her legs. She felt him tear aside the strip of silk that covered her cunt and then his fingers searched between her moist, satiny cunt-lips, to caress them. She was stunned at such a bold gesture, thrilled by his fingers, and she came, her breathing laboured with lust. Eden wanted for him never to stop; wanted more thrills, more daring sexual adventure. Her heart raced. She was frightened they might be seen, terrified to speak and break the spell of her first intensely erotic experience.

Time hung as if suspended. It felt to Eden as if Marshall's caresses had been going on for an eternity. Over his shoulder, she saw the doorman, Carter, returning to the taxi, presumably to open the door for her. She stiffened and Marshall laughed and removed his hand from beneath her skirt. She watched him lick his fingers and nearly fainted with pride that she should have pleased him so much, should have carried off the sexy situation he had placed her in with such aplomb, that he would make the gesture of wanting to devour her. She had never imagined sex would be so thrilling. Now she wanted it and every new experience.

Marshall placed his hand over her heart and smiled

at its swift beating. He bent forward and kissed her on the cheek, whispering in her ear, 'For as long as we are together, never wear underwear. I want you always open and ready for me, so I can give you the sex you demand. Anywhere, anyplace. God, I find you so hot . . . so sexy.'

With that he moved away from her almost at the very moment that the doorman opened the cab door. Eden could hardly recognise her own voice. It sounded hollow and she spoke to Marshall in barely above a whisper. 'I wish it were tomorrow right now at this moment.'

Even as she said it Eden knew she should have been outraged by his audacity, have run away from the practised seduction. But her lust, her ego, were over-taking her powers of logic. She was incapable of playing hard to get with Marshall Greenspan. She had fallen in love and was convinced that he had too.

Eden went to Leila after dinner on the evening of her taxi adventure with Marshall. She watched her mother change her dress to go out with Teddy and her latest admirer.

'Mom, I have a date tomorrow night with Marshall Greenspan.'

Leila turned round from looking in her dressing-table mirror and faced her daughter. She stretched out her arms and Eden walked over to be embraced. 'He's very attractive, Eden. You've made a good choice there. He's intelligent and charming and very sexy. But he's a bounder with women. If you want to go out with him, you must promise me not to let him break your heart.

Do you think you can manage that? If you can, I imagine you'll have a very good time with him. If you can't, my advice as a mother and a woman is not to get involved.

'You're young and beautiful and being caught up with a man like Marshall Greenspan in an affair of the heart will colour your life for relationships with other men who will inevitably follow. Caution, Eden dear. Love, especially being "in love", can hurt if you allow it to. Some women do. I never did, and you must not. That's the best bit of advice I can offer.'

With that Leila stood up and gathered Eden to her, kissing her. 'How exciting! First love, first passion. I can hear it in your voice, see it in your eyes. Make it the best time of your life, my dear girl. One never forgets a first love.'

Eden was immensely touched by her mother's joy for her, and her advice. It was at that moment that she understood what a truly remarkable woman Leila was. Together mother and daughter went to Eden's room and chose the dress she would wear on her first date with Marshall. It was a red, solidly sequined mini-dress with slim shoestring straps over the shoulders. With it she'd wear black fishnet stockings and high-heeled black satin pumps. Mother and daughter decided there'd be no jewellery: Eden's youth and beauty were more impressive than any bauble. They were both aware how seductive and sexy Eden looked and it was then that she understood that Leila accepted that from that night on her daughter was no longer a girl but a young woman entering a new stage in her life.

* * *

Eden rose from her bed and went down to the kitchen to make herself a cup of tea. Winkie and Wonkie leapt from the floor on to her lap as she sat waiting for the kettle to boil. She petted her dogs and thought how right her mother had been. How her first love, or more accurately her first sexual encounter and falling in love, had always remained in her being. She still loved Marshall though she had not seen him for more than forty years and he was a long time dead. Oh, to live again the thrill of sexual madness, lust beyond measure and being totally in love with a man all at the same time. The very thought of it, the memory, brought a smile to Eden's lips, made her heart skip a beat for the joy of first love and passion. Memory had long ago dulled the pain that went along with her in-love state and an erotic life with Marshall. Now more than ever she had to admit to herself that pain had never been inflicted by Marshall but by herself alone. She had agonised over his phone calls, been a young and greedy ego demanding his total attention and devotion. All she had needed to do was to walk away when he did not give her what she craved. But now in retrospect all the pain she had suffered, no matter how bad it had been or who had inflicted it, had been worthwhile. She would not have missed that first love affair with Marshall Greenspan for anything.

Eden stood up from the kitchen table and Winkie and Wonkie slid off her lap on to the floor. They followed her into the music room. Chekov, asleep in a wing chair, raised his head to greet them and then lazily flopped back into a doze. Eden sat down at the piano and thumbed through several pages she had been working on: a composition commissioned by Princeton University on behalf of an anonymous donor. But she could not stay focused on the music. Her mind wandered back to that first sexual experience.

Eden was aware of her own sensual good looks and how both men and women appreciated them. Though she never took such attention seriously she did enjoy making heads turn and always rose to the occasion. Both her father and mother were at home when Marshall called for her. They were charming to him about his taking their daughter out and created an easy atmosphere for Eden, realising from the first moment she greeted Marshall that she was passionately in love with him.

He was dazzled by her. She knew it, her parents knew it. Going down in the lift he told her, 'You look glorious – so sensual. I hate the very idea of sharing you even a little. I want to sweep you away to some secluded place and make love to you. But you know that, don't you?'

'Yes,' she answered because she did know it and that was just what she wanted.

'Later,' he whispered in her ear.

They remained silent for the remainder of the ride down to the ground floor. Sexual tension was building between them and the excitement was so powerful they lost themselves in it.

In the waiting taxi were two men friends of Marshall's. Attractive, dangerously sexy, and quite dazzled by his new young thing, they flirted outrageously with her. Eden was not so much offended by their innuendoes, their occasional kissing of her hand or patting of her knee, the slight graze across her breast, as the fact that the man she was in love with allowed it, even sanctioned it with a smile for his friends and an announcement to her: 'Pay no attention, Eden. They're jealous, furious that I should have discovered you before them.' With that he kissed her on the lips and caressed her face.

For Eden, every hour at that party was a year. As much fun as it was, and studded with celebrities who took her up, men who made passes, women who looked at her with envy, when at last Marshall whispered, 'I've had enough. We're out of here,' the party being over was the best thing about it.

They took a romantic walk down the darkened streets from upper Fifth Avenue to his apartment on Sixty-seventh Street between Madison and Fifth Avenues in a turn-of-the-century brownstone house with a large garden. The interior comprised several large rooms furnished minimally in the modern style. The paintings were Abstract Expressionist. The lighting was impressive and sexy, only the paintings fully lit while a spot recessed in the ceiling poured light on to a drafting table which stood facing the garden.

Marshall switched on music, Sibelius, and removed her coat, dropping it on the floor. He took her by the hand and together they walked up the curved staircase, he leading, Eden following. It all seemed terribly adult and romantic to her. Marshall had such confidence, such self-assurance, she sensed she was in the safest of hands, considering herself lucky that a man such as he was to be her first sexual experience.

'I share this flat with my associate. We work downstairs, entertain there and sleep up here. Fortunately he's away for the night and we have the place to ourselves. That's his room, this is mine.'

With that he opened a door and they stepped into a large room overlooking the garden. There was a massive bed covered with a suede-lined fur blanket. Otherwise the room was bare. Marshall pulled the blanket back to reveal wrinkled white linen sheets. From a cupboard he retrieved pillows and tossed them on to the bed.

Eden was confused. The romance seemed to have vanished though the excitement was still there. She felt awkward, suddenly aware of how inexperienced she was in sexual love. She simply did not know what to do. Marshall undressed hurriedly before her and Eden was astounded by how handsome and virile he was. She was mesmerised by the size and girth of his erect penis, the passion in his eyes for her, desire, lust as she had only imagined it might be. He was rampant and ready for her and she was frozen, not with terror but with anxiety that she might disappoint him, that sex with her might be less than pure bliss. That was what she was ready for, what her heart and body and soul cried out for.

She wore no undergarments and when he raised her dress over her head and dropped it to the floor, he smiled. She had obeyed him. He kissed her breasts and licked her skin and caressed her cunt with searching fingers. He was delighted with her raunchy look: naked save for the black net stockings and high-heeled shoes. Eden promised much with her seductive looks and what to Marshall was obvious hunger to be riven until she screamed for mercy.

And scream and shout and cry with the pain and the pleasure of his animal lust for her, she did. To feel Marshall deep inside her, to sense the power of the pleasure she was giving him, was overwhelming. He wrung from her orgasm after orgasm in quick succession and she lost herself in their lust for each other. Eden wanted this sexual bliss to go on forever.

Marshall mastered her with sex. It was giving her a new dimension of herself and she liked the passion he inspired in her, even though she hardly knew what to do with it. When he exploded and she felt the rush of his hot come she called out his name and sucked hard to hold every drop of his semen within her. They had been a marvellous experience together. Or so she thought until, holding her in his arms, he told her: 'You were delicious but a cheat. You should have told me you were a virgin. That I was to be your first.'

'I didn't know how,' she answered him, somewhat fearful of his tone of voice.

'Not coming on to me as if sex was a second skin you wear might have been a start.'

'Does it matter?' she asked, pulling away from him, heart racing with fear and disappointment at his behaviour.

'Of course it matters. I don't like breaking in young

women. Other men might thrill to that, I don't. I like my women to be ladies in the street and whores in my bed. Women who are experienced in sex and lust and love sex for the erotic life it affords them. I like them to be able to transport me into a sexual life that sizzles and burns deep. I thrive on exploring the dark, animal lust that an erotic world can afford me. We were a case of mistaken identity, you and I. You were as divine as you could be under the circumstances.'

Marshall pulled her back into his arms and caressed her hair. She told him, 'I have fallen in love with you.'

'Bad idea and you have not. You have fallen in love with sex.'

Chapter 3

Eden slipped into her wax-proofed Barbour and, calling
the dogs, set out for a long walk with them in the wood
surrounding her house. She kept thinking about the
love affair she had pursued with Marshall. He had not
wanted it, she had. She had been desperate to find love
in the erotic life they shared. He became her mentor in
sex but never in love. All these years later she could
understand what she had refused to believe when they
were together: he simply did not love her in the same
way she loved him, and he never had. Yet they remained
lovers in an on again, off again fashion for years. They
had even very nearly become friends.

She had had youth and beauty and enormous talent
on her side, and in time enough admirers to dull the
blow of not being loved by Marshall Greenspan. Eden
was quite shocked to think that even now, a near lifetime ago, having lost him to another woman still left a
bruise around her heart. She raised her chin that little
bit higher and said aloud, 'Thank you, God, for
Marshall and the erotic passion he had for me. For

allowing myself to be moulded sexually by him.'

She began to laugh at herself, one of her many endearing traits, and broke into a run through the wood, the dogs chasing after her. How good it felt still, in these autumn years of her life, to love her lovers. She ran all the way back to the house feeling a new kind of freedom. The joy of admitting to love and passion, of wallowing in it rather than cutting it out of her life as she had done for so many years.

Once more in the house, the dogs dried off and huddling with her in front of the open fire, she gave in to her desperate need to return to the world where she had been such a sexual success, where she had been so enriched by her lovers, had been so young, vital and happy. Suddenly the very idea of travelling to those places excited her. She sensed that being there would validate what a marvellous erotic life she had lived there, that time had not transformed the actual into a flight of the imagination.

She had not forgotten her troubling state of sexual invisibility and that she was no longer the person she'd thought she was. Walking over to the drinks tray, she opened a chilled split of champagne and filled her glass. Pol Roger White Label had been Churchill's favourite champagne; it was hers as well. She felt buoyed by the taste, the sense of occasion. She would close the house the very next day and strut back once more into the world she had walked away from.

The housekeeper was called before Eden even finished her glass of champagne. Rachel would move in to take care of things here. Eden's next call was to Max Kerwood, her agent of more than twenty years. She experienced momentary anxiety before the tone stopped and he was on the line.

'I'm going away, Max.'

'For how long, where and why?' he asked, sensing at once that something important had happened.

'You should have told me I was turning into one of the millions of invisible women,' she chided him.

'Why should I? You only needed to look in the mirror to see what you were doing to yourself. I thought that was what you wanted – to leave the stage, become a recluse, concentrate on composing rather than performing? Have sex with the occasional country gent, the gardener, anything that didn't interfere with the passion in your soul.'

'Max, I've been having a good hard look at what my erotic life has been and what it is at present. I don't like what I see. I seem to have neglected that side of my life. Where did it go? And why did I let it? It's not that I'm going all out to find love or a new erotic life for myself, more that I want to revisit my favourite places and remember what it once was to be an erotic soul there in search of love, passion of the heart. I have to know if I have really become a poor shadow of the woman I once was. Have I burned myself out as attractive and sensual in the eyes of vital, exciting men? Am I now entering another phase of my life, where I'll begin a new way of being and loving? Who knows? Certainly not me. Hence I'm taking a sabbatical and going on an adventure. I'm not prepared meekly to accept being one of the invisible women men no longer look at, let alone want. I want more than that.'

'Do you know where you're going first?' a by now fascinated Max asked.

'To open the house in Hydra. I'll start from there, my beloved Greece. Could you be a dear and transfer some money into my Athens account?'

'And I'll call Maria and tell her to open the house. It must be ages since you've been there. And so long since the concert you gave in Syntagma Square, the amphitheatre in Epidaurus. I always thought you were crazy to hang on to your property in Hydra. Now suddenly it makes sense that you insisted on keeping it. When should I tell Maria you will be there?'

'Two days' time. Book me for one night at the Grande Bretagne in Athens. And no PR, Max. This is a very personal odyssey and though I'm taking my cello, I have no intention of performing in public.'

'I hear you. How long do you expect to be in Greece?'

'I have no idea. But I'll keep you in the picture of where I am and what I'm doing.'

'You sound happier than I've heard you in a very long time,' he told her.

Max was at Heathrow Airport when Eden arrived. She was not surprised. He had a history of taking care of her and they both knew that was the way it would always be. He never failed to be where he had to be in order to make her way easier, dismissing the mundanities of travel and life in general for Eden. He saw that as his privilege.

She saw him immediately she arrived at the terminal. Hardly a woman who passed him did not give him a second glance. Max was over six foot tall with broad shoulders and film star good looks. He was dressed in a belted crisp-looking Burberry, collar turned up. Dark blond hair prematurely streaked with white and worn on the long side framed his strong perfect features. For the first time in all the years she had known him Eden realised that he resembled Marshall Greenspan in his good looks and self-assurance.

Max was in love with Eden. He knew it and had declared it nearly twenty years before. And Eden loved Max. The tragedy or success of their love affair, depending on how one looked at it, was that they loved each other in different ways. Max had declared once and never again that he would marry no woman except her, and he never had. Instead he had mistresses and three children to whom he was a great father but remained besotted by Eden.

Walking across the crowded terminal towards him now she was reminded of how much discipline it had taken not to have a sexual relationship with Max. The desire had been there for both of them but set aside from year to year, not the thing to indulge themselves in when business was and would always be the lion's share of their affair.

So many times they had come close to consummating their love-business affair with sex: one moonlit night in Sorrento, after a concert in Paris, on a yacht sailing up the Nile. But always Eden had pulled back. Now decades had passed as had other lovers and they were still together in all but lust. She sensed once more she had been right. Their relationship was the sweeter and the more exciting, always fresh, for the way they had dealt with it.

Max was looking in the opposite direction when she approached him. Eden touched his cheek with the back of her hand, they smiled and kissed, and with Max slipping his arm through hers they walked to the check-in desk followed by a porter with her cello.

'Everything is arranged,' Max told her, showing his VIP visitor's pass as they walked to the first-class lounge where they had a glass of champagne. 'Don't do anything foolish.'

'Have you ever known me to be?' she asked.

'Never,' he told her, admiration in his voice.

'It's because I am not a foolish woman that I am making this odyssey. Surely you can understand that?'

He walked her to the departure gate and super-intended the transfer of her cello which would travel in the seat next to her. They kissed goodbye and he was gone without another word. Max had been paving an easy way for Eden for so long they both took it for granted. These were the roles they played in each other's lives and things would never change. What was so incredible was that at no time did either of them ever abuse the situation.

Once he was gone Eden put him thoroughly out of her mind, still preoccupied with her own invisibility. The incident in Frog's Hollow had badly undermined her confidence and goaded her into action. She felt she had no option but to begin again. Invisibility was too unrewarding.

As the plane circled Athens Eden's heart skipped a beat: the sprawling white of the houses covered the landscape as far as the blue of the Aegean, the winter sun beating down giving an added sparkle to the sight. No matter how often Eden flew over the city it always remained something marvellous in her heart and mind. A unique place with heart and soul that no matter how it grew remained always charmingly provincial for all its attempted sophistication.

Now, with the descent of the plane, she understood how right she was to have made this trip, to see once again the beauty of the places she had experienced in her youth and remember her lovers there. It was a validation of the thrilling and adventurous life lived. By no means was she in search of another man nor the return of a sexual life to make herself feel complete, desirable. She was looking for something more than that.

As she descended the stairs to walk across the tarmac to the terminal Eden realised that she was about to have a very good time. A fun time. Something she had not been having for many years because she had, for whatever reason, abandoned her will to do so. Almost aloud she muttered, 'Fuck that woman's plague of growing invisible with age,' and wondered how she had ever allowed herself to fall into the middle-age trap.

Halfway between the plane and the terminal, she recognised Andoni Pappas rushing across the tarmac to greet her. She placed her cello on the ground just in time for him to crush her in a huge embrace, tears of pleasure filling his eyes. Max, as usual making life as easy as possible for Eden, had quite obviously called on Andoni to take charge of her arrival.

A former Prime Minister and admirer of her genius as one of the world's great cellists, his adoration of her as a woman had never flagged in all the many years they had known each other. He had arranged memorable nights for Eden that he and a handful of selected friends as well would never forget: Eden Sidd playing by moonlight on the steps of the Propylia at the Parthenon; a lazy picnic in the sun at the Temple of Sounion with her playing Bach in an after-lunch interlude where the glorious Aegean sparkling blue below a cloudless sky of the same colour and intensity made it difficult to distinguish, save for the movement of water, where earth separated from sky. Memories came rushing back of the many other places she had been privileged to play, not in concert but for herself: a sunset at Knossos, on a remote deserted island near Ikaria, in Delos one dawn morning, in the courtyard of the monastery high up in Hora Patmos.

The two old friends kissed and as their lips met for a fleeting moment she remembered the lovers who had afterwards rounded off such splendid experiences. Garfield Barton, handsome and sexual, filled her

thoughts. She pushed him firmly from her mind as she
stroked Andoni's cheek with the back of her hand. He
had been one of the many who had tried to make her
wrench Garfield from her heart. Even now as Andoni
and she looked at each other she could remember the
anxiety he'd felt for her in her desperate love then.

Arms wrapped around each other, Andoni and Eden
broke away from the queue snaking its way into the
terminal and walked to the waiting car where one of his
faithful attendants took Eden's passport and slipped
away to process her entry into the country.

The warmth and charm of Greeks was always a
pleasant surprise for Eden. She and Andoni had not
seen each other for years and yet they spoke as if they
had been in touch constantly. Eden felt suddenly in
touch with herself and the world and very much more
alive and happy.

The traffic from the terminal into the centre of Athens
was more congested and chaotic than ever. A cloud of
pollution hung over the city, something she had not
seen before. But the vitality and noise and bizarre
driving, the blocks of modern concrete apartment
buildings with mean little balconies, were in much the
same style as she remembered.

'Progress has a great deal to answer for,' she said to
Andoni.

'Everywhere, my dear, not only in Greece,' he replied.
'Max said I should not impose hospitality on you, or
anything else for that matter. A very private, very
personal journey was what he called your visit. So I

hesitate to ask you to dine with us this evening . . .'

'He told it to you the way it is, Andoni. You will forgive me if I decline?'

'Let me at least offer you my boat to take you to your island.'

Andoni's schooner was a familiar sight in Hydra. It was probably the most low-key return she could hope for and so without hesitation she accepted his offer.

Andoni was surprised as the car drew up before the Grande Bretagne when Eden asked him not even to accompany her into the hotel. Surprised but not offended. He watched as the doorman greeted her and removed the cello from her hands. He knew her, of course, as did most of the hotel's staff from the years of her love affair with Greece, her fame as a musician and as the lover of the American painter Garfield Barton.

Eden went directly into the streets of Athens after registering in the hotel and instructing the concierge to send up toothbrush and paste. Except for her cello and her handbag she had travelled with no luggage. She was an old hand at travelling, always wearing just the right sort of clothes so that she would be chic and well dressed no matter where she was going or not going as the case might be. Today she had chosen a fine herringbone tweed dress of charcoal grey and over her shoulders a suede jacket lined in silver fox, with large revers of the fur framing her face. Black high-heeled alligator shoes matched her Hermès handbag.

She had forgotten the way the Greeks conduct their lives in the streets and was delighted by the crowds rushing about. She realised after no more than a few minutes how much she had missed the Greek need to play at life, enjoy the leisure of long lunches and siestas, their inability to stay at home and be bored. She laughed aloud as she walked through the familiar streets and memories of the past came flooding in on her.

Eden stopped at some of the old haunts where she had drunk with her friends of an afternoon. At Kolanaki, a square where everyone met to sit and watch the world go by over endless cups of coffee, ouzo or whisky, waiters recognised her and made a fuss over her return. Eden was enjoying herself but was relieved that she had not run into any old friends. She wandered the familiar streets alone and at ease with herself.

In Plaka, she returned as she had done hundreds of times to one of the old tavernas where she was recognised by the owner and made to feel welcome. He behaved as if the absence since she had dined with them had been nothing more than a short interlude. She sat alone and dined on stuffed vine leaves, roasted peppers and aubergines, pan fried squid, a grilled fish smothered in herbs and lemon, and too much wine. Strangers at the next table raised their glasses in toasts to her and, finding it unbearable that she should be dining alone, tried to convince her to join them. Eden was saved by the tactful proprietor and they finally accepted she was not lonely for company. She sent a bottle of wine to their table and shook hands with them before leaving the restaurant to return to her hotel.

Walking back from Plaka Eden was overcome with

thankfulness that she had had the courage to step back in time and reassess the beauty and passion that had once been in her life. She understood that there was much work to be done now in order to live as fully as she had once done, chances to be taken. She would be fully visible once more.

But where did she begin? Not by looking for a man, sexual affairs, love, she was certain of that. And even more so when she entered the Grande Bretagne and heads turned in admiration of this beautiful, vibrant woman with a clear will to be visible to the world, one who demanded to be seen and admired. She was quite stunned at the vision she saw of herself as she passed a long mirror. Stunned enough to stop and admire herself. She laughed aloud then and walked from the lobby to the nearly deserted bar where she ordered a champagne cocktail and raised her glass in a silent toast to new beginnings.

Eden's mind slid back and she remembered another time in this bar. It had been a sunny afternoon in spring and she was there with an American writer, Charles Halderman, who'd thought she might like to meet Gore Vidal. That was the way Athens was then, writers and painters constantly passing through. It had been so easy to meet the famous, the talented and successful. In those days people were generous with introductions as long as you were either beautiful, talented, or someone fancied you as a quickie sexual liaison. Eden had been dazzled by Halderman's talent and charm, and impressed by the fact that he'd had a critical success in London with his first novel. Few who knew him were not.

How naive she had been about meeting the handsome, erudite, successful writer Gore Vidal! She'd thought he would be enchanted by her own youth and beauty, her musical genius, when he had clearly not been. Even now, all these years later, she could remember the look on Vidal's face once he found himself alone with her when Charles had gone to the bar for more drinks. The handsome looks vanished as he hissed at her, 'What are you? Some hanger on – a would-be writer hoping Charles's talent will rub off on you? He doesn't want you, haven't you figured that out?'

Clearly neither did Gore Vidal. He found her presence an intrusion and she remembered all these years later how she'd stood her ground with the literary man until Charles's return and then made a dignified exit, smarting and concerned that he just might be right about her. Alone now, drinking her champagne cocktail, she came to terms with the truth. Though he had been wrong about her desire to be a writer Gore Vidal had been right on all the other counts.

Charles was now dead and long-forgotten. His was a flash-in-the-pan success whereas hers had been bright and consistent. As for Gore Vidal, he was as he had always been a name to reckon with in literary circles. His was a talent that went from strength to strength. Intelligent, articulate, outspoken and oh, so clever, she could now understand why he couldn't be bothered to be civil to her way back then. She had been unformed, searching for recognition and passionate love. What had that to do with men such as Halderman and Vidal? It had to do only with her and her own ambitions, she knew that now. How had it taken so many years for her to face her own egoism and ambition? Her passion for music had blinded her to so many other things in her life.

In the lift going up to her room there were two other passengers, a French couple. The man was attentive to his partner but before they emerged from the lift, he looked Eden over and smiled at her. It was a sensual smile. An unmistakably come-hither look passed between them as their eyes met.

Chapter 4

To sail from Piraeus to Hydra on board Andoni's schooner was for Eden a joy she would never forget. To see the islands basking in the winter sun of the Aegean – white rambling houses for the most part built on barren rock, only the occasional dot and dash of green trees – was for her sheer poetry. What she saw reached into her soul and engulfed the past. On this voyage of return what she was seeing was more rich and exciting than Eden's fondest memories of her beloved Greek Islands.

When on her first visit to Greece she had seen Aegina lying in the middle of the Saronic Gulf, the first of the small chain of islands closest to Athens, she had been dazzled by the simplicity and romance of it, so quiet and serene in its unadorned beauty. It had been the first stop of the ferry taking her further on to Hydra. She had been exhausted from a tour and had wanted, needed, to get away from her work and her life.

The ferry had only stopped for a few minutes and she had watched half a dozen Greeks, several men and one woman draped in black pulling along a crying child.

Bundles had been tossed down on to the quay, men instantly hard at work loading them on donkeys. The boat sailed away long before the shouting of the men and the screeching of the donkeys subsided.

Eden's thoughts flashed forward to the second time she'd seen Aegina. She smiled to herself at the memory. By that time she'd been swept off her feet by Garfield. How in love they had been. Loving him and making him happy had become the focus of her life. Their sexual life together took them over and blinded Eden, made her deaf to all warnings, even those signs she saw herself.

Skylark, Andoni's schooner, so black and sleek and glorious to look at with its burnt orange-coloured sails billowing in the wind, passed close to Aegina but did not stop. At Poros, the next island on, *Skylark* was just ahead of the ferry. Eden could see the vendors waiting for the boat to dock and the passengers to rush off to buy pistachios and rush on board again before it pulled away. *Skylark* swooped in close to the quay and the captain tossed a bag of coins to one of the vendors who tossed back plastic bags of the nuts into the waiting hands of the crew leaning over the schooner's railings. Good-natured laughter and banter rang out as they sailed on towards Hydra.

Standing at the *Skylark*'s prow eating pistachios, the wind colder than the sunlight promised, Eden huddled into her fox collar while her old life flooded back to her and her soul began to rise again from the doldrums of invisibility. It was late-afternoon when *Skylark* dropped anchor in Hydra. The sun was still high in the sky and the port quiet, just awakening from siesta and making ready for its night life. The sight of white houses and narrow cobblestone streets winding their way from the crescent-shaped port right to the top of the hill behind made Eden's heart race with the pleasure of return. The bell in the tower struck up its familiar sound and the water lapping against the moored boats was a symphony to Eden's ears. She recognised every house and pictured its inhabitants, every shop, taverna and cafe, but her eyes settled not on her own house, a short climb away, but on Garfield's. The shutters were closed, he was not in residence. Not that that affected her one way or another.

Eden found it strange that she recognised no one in the sleepy port. The people around seemed so young, so attractive, so glossy. They glanced at her with momentary curiosity, nothing lasting or meaningful. There was even a tinge of indifference. Not at all like the old days when she had been a part of the Hydra scene.

One of the many tourist shops that had sprung up since her departure was just opening its doors. Eden stopped and bought a pair of sandals. Carrying her shoes in one hand and her cello in the other, she left the port to begin the climb to her house, which she could now see clearly. A chain of donkeys clip-clopped past her and their owner stopped and greeted her.

The years had been good to Petros. The donkey man and Eden recognised each other at once and exchanged greetings. Then he insisted on loading the cello on to Evangelia, and Eden on to Despina, and gave them a ride to her house. The Greeks have never been famed for their subtlety. He asked as many intimate questions as he could get in before they reached the walls surrounding her house and garden. There he called out and the housekeeper appeared almost at once to greet Eden.

Petros followed her into the courtyard carrying her cello. The donkeys remained outside on the narrow path between the high walls surrounding neighbouring houses. No one ever offended Petros or any of the other donkey carriers; they were the only mode of transportation on the island and everyone was dependent on them. The housekeeper, Maria, had to wipe away tears of joy at seeing Eden again. She insisted Petros remain for an Ouzo and some pieces of freshly roasted octopus which she had arranged on a table under the spreading fig tree now barren of leaves and fruit.

Eden's house had originally been a series of small houses she had bought years ago as they came on the market. She had completed her rambling conversion twelve years before and now marvelled that the view from its terraces as they gently climbed up the hill, tier upon tier, still remained one of the best the island had to offer. From here she could see the port below her and the houses to the right and left, filling the crescent of the hillside.

At last she was alone to walk through the rooms, familiarising herself with them again. Eden had forgotten how much she loved this house. All the shutters were open and it was flooded with light. The light of Greece, even late-afternoon winter light – there is nothing in the world like it. The rooms were all painted white and furnished minimally. Every chair, table, painting, sculpture was a thing of beauty set in a space that would only enhance it. The largest of the rooms was near to being perfect in proportion, a double cube, and in it were set a pair of Bechstein pianos. Eden approached them and struck a few notes on each. They were in perfect tune. A piano tuner from Athens arrived twice a year, year in and year out, to see that they remained so.

She was reminded of the excitement and drama of getting these pianos into her house. The entire island had turned out for the event. They had been manhandled up here under the direction of Petros the donkey man, a dozen of his friends and workers. Garfield had organised it. No matter that her Greek was better than his, and her anxiety over the instruments more acute, he had taken charge as the men would listen to him. That was something she as a woman could not achieve. The islanders, like everyone else, adored Garfield. He had been one of the first foreigners to buy a house here. The short dark Greeks were in awe of the tall handsome wide-shouldered American with his sandy blond hair. Even more so of the stream of important visitors who arrived on their island to stay with him.

They respected his being a painter, living on little money while awaiting fame and fortune. Then when Eden arrived on the island and was swept off her feet by the charm and sexuality of Garfield Barton, the islanders took the romance to their own hearts and thought the more of him for having captured such a beauty, so glamorous and famous. Eden's and Garfield's had been a romance that everyone admired, envied. They had been the beautiful people, worldly, who came and went from the island in dramatic romantic meetings and partings: Eden sailing away leaving her love behind to paint and enjoy the seclusion and simplicity of life on Hydra while she toured the world dazzling audiences with her brilliance on the cello.

Occasionally their paths would cross elsewhere when Garfield would leave the island to hustle the art dealers of Paris, London and New York. In New York together, they frequented the cultured circles that appreciated great musicians and painters on the make for stardom. They were creative celebrities with an instant entrée to any party where art met fun head on and the exchange of ideas was heady as the strongest perfume. Adrenaline was in the air and one breathed deep of it to stay alive and in tune with the whirl of New York on the make.

Garfield was the love of Eden's life. She was flattered by his attentions, his love, their sex life together. She believed totally his sad tales of how he had been taken advantage of by a crippled wife, a French countess with a famous bitch of a mother who had promised the young couple the world and had delivered a great deal less than Garfield expected. The so-called crippled wife (nothing more than a rheumatic heart) had turned out to be as strong a character as the mother and completely in love with Garfield whom she turned into nothing less than a servant to any and all of her needs. It had been said he used her title as an entrée to the rich and famous of European aristocracy while she used him as a decorative crutch and her introduction to the Bohemian world of artists and writers.

By the time Eden had met Garfield he had dumped his first wife but only after having received a substantial settlement, a small flat in Paris and the huge and magnificent house in Hydra. The scandalmongers claimed he was able to get such a settlement because he'd threatened to expose publicly what everyone gossiped about: the mother had been enchanted with Garfield, had had him first for a lover and then married him off to the daughter to keep him in the family.

Eden made herself deaf to such gossip, blind to any aspects of his character that were less than admirable. In New York she watched him hustle the rich ladies who collect paintings, watched him play the role of single, eligible, handsome painter. He put up a great front, saying that he was staying with an old friend and not Eden who was just a passing fancy. Yet everyone knew she was something important in his life.

Garfield Barton was a high-society American gigolo who painted fashionable subjects. He labelled himself artist and the world was charmed by him and his work. Smooth and ingratiating he used himself rather than his talent to climb the art ladder and win the friendship of some of the great painters of their time.

Eden believed him to be a good artist who loved her. In all the years she was passionately devoted to him she could never bring herself to accept that he was the gigolo other people claimed him to be. He had never taken money off her, used or abused the love they had had when they had been together – or so she maintained to herself and everyone who tried to make her see the affair in its true light.

Hydra had been their haven where the world and Garfield's flaws were left behind. It was difficult to say when Eden faced the truth about their love affair: one glance too many by Garfield at another older woman with a great deal of money, the realisation that she would always be less than the most important person in his life, the moment he walked away from her when she was in crisis and told her he would be back when she'd straightened herself and her career out.

Standing in her house now, all these years later, looking out on his closed shutters was the first time she could admit to herself that she had fooled herself about their love. To her it had been significant whereas to him she had been just like every other woman he had ever had an affair with. That realisation left her feeling free, as if she had dropped a huge stone she had been carrying for decades: the desperate self-delusion of love.

As Eden walked through to the kitchen where she opened a bottle of wine and poured two glasses, one for Maria and one for herself, she took a few minutes to ask herself some questions about her affair with Garfield. How much of it had she created to satisfy her own need to be loved as strongly as she had loved him? Had that love really been the great love of her life as she had once believed it to be? Why had she had to come this far in her life to face the truth when it no longer mattered? And it didn't. She had left him behind more than a decade ago. Never thought of him as a person now, only ever as the abstract embodiment of a great love affair during one of the best times of her life.

After several glasses of wine, Eden settled down to play the cello. Hours passed before she realised she was playing in the dark. Turning on several lamps, she walked through to the upper terrace where her bedroom had been made ready for her. She found a plate of sandwiches and a carafe of water left there by Maria and, lighting the fire, sat in front of it for an hour before she went to bed and slipped into a dream of the stranger who had sent her on this Odyssey of self-discovery.

The next morning she was up bright and early to the sound of the church bell, a cock crowing from some distance above her house, the screech of a donkey and the clip-clop of his hooves on the stones as he passed down the path to the port. She could smell Maria's coffee and frying eggs and bacon.

After breakfast in the garden Eden walked the streets of Hydra. Memories of her sexual excesses with Garfield, and how she had been enriched by them when she had been so young and innocent and happy, flooded back to her. What she had hoped for in revisiting the romantic places of her past, that it might validate her old erotic life, was happening. She had not been fooling herself as she had started to fear she might have done.

The Hydriots did of course remember her but few of the expatriates who lived in Hydra happened to be there at present. These were the months when most of them travelled or returned to their native lands for sentimental reunions with their relations. It was almost as if she had her island to herself and that suited Eden just fine. It allowed memories of her past life to invade the present as she climbed the narrow paths up over the spine of the island.

It was early-evening when she returned to her house. She bathed and changed her clothes and walked down a path towards the port to her favourite taverna. Set in a garden several streets in from the moored fishing boats, it boasted the best Greek cooking on the island. After a bear hug from the proprietor and a turn around the kitchen where she looked into every pot and chose her dinner, Eden sat by the open fire on a rickety wooden chair at a table that wobbled with every slash of the knife as she cut the roast lamb on her chipped white plate.

Well into her meal she was unaware of the man watching her until the table stopped wobbling and she looked up to see who it was who had fixed the offending leg. He straightened up and Eden felt a glow of happiness warm her through and through. It had been years since she had seen handsome Sebastian Morrell. He was still, in his late-sixties, a big man in every way. Time had not bowed him. Tragedy had not marked him. Ever since that first day she had met him in Alexandria she had known that his good looks, charm, the openness with which he lived, his appetite for adventure and will to live life to the fullest, were too strong for her to handle in any relationship but strictly no strings attached for either of them. He had been in those heady days of youth a womaniser, irresistible to women. She could see that nothing had changed. She wanted him now as she had wanted him then. She had not envisaged accidentally encountering one of her old lovers on her travels but here was one in the flesh.

They smiled at each other. He raised her hand and lowered his head to kiss it. She was aware that whatever the years had brought him, Sebastian had not changed. His entire life was still bound up with the sexual passion he loved to arouse in others. His sheer physical presence was overwhelming: the strong, masculine, Greek god-like face. He was like the more-than-life-size bronze statue of Poseidon, absurdly powerful, as if he too had just risen from the sea. It had been too long since Eden had felt the dynamism of such a man.

'You look as lovely as ever. But I would have expected that of you,' he told her.

Without asking he took the empty chair at her table and moved it round to sit next to Eden.

'Sebastian – so many years. I can hardly believe we're sitting here together.'

'You came to Hydra and didn't expect to see me? I've never really left the island. Yes, I've lived in other places for work, for the sake of my wife and daughter, but my heart was always here. It always will be.'

'How are Betty and your daughter? Are they here with you?'

'Betty and I made a big mistake but out of it I gained

my daughter, something better than marvellous. I love her with all my heart though she's dead now, and with her part of me died. So I returned here to Hydra to live out what's left of my life. Marisol would understand that. I never lied to either her or Betty.'

Eden thought about Betty who had trapped Sebastian into marriage with her pregnancy and suffered tortures from his infidelities ever afterwards. That had been their deal. He had lived as he wanted to live, adored his daughter, played the part of husband for a few months of the year to keep Betty quiet. She knew it, as did everyone who knew about that marriage, even though he had been discreet and never flaunted his private life in his wife's face.

Eden wanted to bite out her tongue for having asked after them. She had in fact heard that his adored child, Marisol, had committed suicide while Sebastian was in the Far East on business. No one had had the slightest idea that she had been depressed or unhappy. No note had been left. Her death broke Sebastian's heart. It was the tragedy of his life. He left Rome where they had lived then and retreated to Hydra. He also left Betty who, when she learned he was making a life without her in Greece, promptly committed suicide, using the same gun their daughter had. That was eighteen months ago. Eden had even sent a note of condolence to Sebastian at the time of Marisol's tragic death. But seeing him unexpectedly, the years had rolled back and she had momentarily forgotten what had happened.

'Why has it taken you so long to return here to your

lovely house, your beautiful things?' asked Sebastian.

'I don't know. I think I got swallowed up by the life I thought I had to have. I allowed myself to be sold a bill of goods about growing old, gracefully slipping out of the limelight of success before I was defeated by younger or more beautiful women on the make. As I once was and am no longer.'

'Lovers?' asked Sebastian.

'Occasional dull ones. Men who have forgotten about the naughty side of their sexual lives – or if they haven't are out there with younger women playing dirty old men and are too cautious with me.'

Sebastian's food arrived and he and Eden finished their meal together through the many interruptions by locals who stopped by to greet them and offer drinks. Sebastian was well loved by the Hydriots and seeing him with Eden started tongues wagging. They thought of Sebastian as the stud of the island for there were not many foreign women who arrived in Hydra and left without him bedding them. That counted for a great deal with the Greeks, both men and women, who either envied Sebastian or yearned after him.

Sebastian insisted that Eden and he go to the port to one of the cafes for a night cap. She did not need too much persuasion. Being with him had rolled back the years; the sheer charm and sexiness of the man rubbed off him and on to her. He was a master of seduction and it felt so good to Eden she could think of nothing else but the joy, the sheer delight, of being wooed for sex and satisfaction by a handsome stud like Sebastian.

They left the cafe arm in arm and walked round the crescent-shaped port, past the fishing boats bobbing up and down in the water. They listened to the sound of the waves slapping against the wooden hulls, the quiet of the night, and were embraced by a nearly full moon and a black sky strewn with bright twinkling stars. Away from the port they climbed through the narrow streets of cobblestones and whitewashed walls and stopped to kiss. Several kisses later their hunger for each other peaked and Sebastian picked Eden up in his arms and carried her the rest of the way to his house.

Eden, overwhelmed by his passion for her, was naked to the waist by the time he carried her over the threshold. His hands roamed over her breasts and she felt herself melting with desire to be ravaged by Sebastian. That was the way he made love to women: by ravaging them with his lust for all things erotic, not with love and tenderness.

Sebastian recognised Eden's sexual hunger and that for him was always an aphrodisiac in a woman. It was in haste that he climbed out of his clothes and stood naked in front of Eden, tantalising her with his body. So firm and masculine, so rampant with lust. He was a joy to look at, to touch. She caressed him with searching hands and kissed his flesh, licked it, nibbled on his nipples, rubbed her face across his chest, caressed his buttocks and slipped her finger down the crack that divided its muscular cheeks. The look of pleasure on his face drove her on to take his erect phallus into her mouth and deep into her throat while she caressed his ample testes.

Until Sebastian, Eden had forgotten how much she missed a man such as he, how much she missed lust, sex unbound.

Sebastian quite suddenly had had enough. He swept Eden off her feet and carried her to his bed. There he placed her on her knees facing away from him and took her in one fell swoop. He thrust deeply into her and fucked her with long and steady movements that gave her maximum pleasure, while he caressed her breasts and bottom, kissed the back of her neck and sucked on her ear lobes. Eden had multiple orgasms that came swiftly one after the other and called out to the heavens from the pain of such exquisite pleasure.

Chapter 5

She was still asleep when Sebastian arrived with a breakfast tray: scrambled eggs, bacon, hot coffee, a bowl of preserved peaches, a stack of buttered toast. He awakened her with a brief kiss on the cheek, arranged the tray and then, dropping his robe, carefully slipped into bed next to her.

He poured the coffee, hers black, his half coffee and half hot milk.

Eden watched how adroitly he managed the two liquids at the same time: the stream of black and white as they merged in the bottom of the cup. 'I'd forgotten that you take your breakfast coffee like a Frenchman,' she told him.

'But I had not forgotten you take yours black. Why would you remember? It's not as if we had that many breakfasts together. You were always afraid to stay the night. I never could understand that. An adventurer in all things erotic with me but unable to walk from my house in daylight.'

'Quite simple. I didn't want the island to know I was

61

another sexual notch on your belt.'

'But that wasn't the case with Garfield.'

'No. Well, he and I were in love. That's quite a different thing,' Eden told Sebastian as she forked scrambled egg into her mouth.

'I was in lust for you and that's another kind of love. My "in lust" is in its way as powerful as the love you sought with Garfield. Just different. Last night is a case in point. While we were in the throes of intense erotic pleasure, you were the only woman in the world for me. At that moment we shared a love as pure as any you ever had with another man. I have no doubt about that whether you want to admit it or not. It's true.

'For a few hours, I was the only man, the only love, you wanted. The kind of sex we had is everything because I know how to reach down to the basic instinct in a woman where it all begins and ends. For a few hours together we made the entire world, with all its goodness, its badness, its emotional domination of our lives, fall away. What other act can do that and also give such pleasure, transform the here and now into another dimension where one can live in pure ecstasy, sheer bliss, with no strings attached?'

Eden watched Sebastian raise his coffee cup to his lips and sip as he looked over its rim into her eyes. He was right, of course, and his words and the fact that she believed them quite surprised her. For all the years she had known him she had never given him credit for understanding his own voracious appetite for sex, the compulsive need to fuck every desirable woman who appeared before him. Had she been such a hypocrite as to believe she had not used him as a stud herself? Most of the women she knew who had been to bed with Sebastian had done the same after all. But what of the many who'd labelled their lust for him love?

A question ran through Eden's mind as she accepted a peach half off the silver spoon Sebastian was feeding her from. The flavour burst like a sparkling firework in her mouth and her taste buds ran wild with pleasure, distracting her from wondering if it was possible that all those years with Garfield had been spent in love as justification for lust, for her own need to love and be loved at any price? It didn't bear thinking of. Whatever it was, it was in the past and no longer mattered. Eden was in search of life and the present. As Sebastian caressed her breasts and offered her her cup of coffee, she was aware that he was never going to be a part of her life in any way other than a source of sex when she was available and he wanted her. Sebastian did wonders for her ego and her invisibility but he was not what she was looking for, though he made a good beginning.

It was as if he'd been reading her mind when he asked, 'What are you looking for, Eden? Why are you here?'

Sebastian had never been the sort of man Eden would confide in and so it surprised her when she told him about the crisis she was going through. She followed it up with her story of the stranger in the tea room. Sebastian's reaction was to throw back his head and laugh.

'You're laughing at me!' she exclaimed, horrified.

He placed his cup and saucer down on the tray. Then, pulling her into his arms, he caressed her hair with both his hands and kissed her full on the lips. She struggled but he was too strong for her and she finally gave in to his kiss and caresses.

When she was calm again in his arms, he released her and told her, 'Yes, I'm laughing at you.'

Then he attacked his plate of scrambled eggs by forking some of them on to a piece of crisp toast. He bit into it and Eden watched him savour every morsel and sip from his coffee cup. He was a joy to watch if for no other reason than his sheer enthusiasm for life's pleasures.

Finally he spoke. 'Women never cease to amaze me. I have met and passed by hundreds, thousands, who were no less invisible than in the scene you just described to me. I never gave them a second glance because they were lost, had given up their sexuality, their passion for lust and coming, exchanged it for some sort of second-rate existence that excluded sex. They wore that expression like a medal of honour, as if they had earned it in the battle of the sexes and won. Part-time or full-time celibacy their reward.

'I could never imagine you, Eden, even contemplating joining that brigade. I would have given you more credit than ever to have allowed yourself to be hoodwinked into retiring to a life so foreign to who and what you are. You were sold the bag of senseless insecurities that comes to women with middle age. Or maybe being in love and lust with Garfield and falling out of it burned you out. Was it one of those decisions women make when they have paid too high a price for love? No, never again the pain, the laying down of one's soul for a bastard to walk over? Better the occasional fuck where you can leave the love and sacrifice out of it. Go for an alternative that delivers peace and quiet, and is a safe house to dwell in.

'Well, for a smart lady you took a wrong turn. You lost your lustre, forgot how good it was to shine and spin the world in your hands. Now pass me that dish of peach halves, my beauty, and I'll suck them from your cunt and you'll love it.'

With that he removed the breakfast tray from the bed and pulled the sheet covering them from the bed.

Several hours later Sebastian walked Eden back to her house and she played the cello for him. Lost in the music of Schubert, she played with a passion that had been missing from her performances for years. She played as she had during the height of her career and was aware that a rebirth of some sort was already happening for her. Eden licked her lips. She could taste the sweetness of the peaches Sebastian had fed from his mouth to hers, and they were all the more succulent because they were tinged with her orgasms. Eden knew that she had been given a second introduction to an erotic world she had missed to the very core of her being. She looked up from her instrument and was not surprised to see that Sebastian was no longer in the room with her. No wonder so many women fall in love with him, she mused. Sebastian Morell always knew when and how to make an exit.

She put her bow down on the music stand and rose from her chair. Stowing her cello in its case, then the bow, she closed it and went to the window from where she saw Sebastian walking slowly down the path leading to the port. Her eye strayed from him to the closed and shuttered house that still belonged to Garfield.

While Eden understood Sebastian and how he felt about love, she could not accept, refused to accept, that the love she'd once had with Garfield had been no more than futile obsession with oblivion its destination. Was she still in love with him, after all the years that had passed? No, she thought not. It was more that she was still in love with being in love with another human being. Of self-sacrifice that was returned threefold by the mere opening up wholly to another human being who loved in the same way in return, no matter the length or brevity of the affair.

That evening Eden dined alone in the port at a restaurant where she and Garfield had shared so many happy and loving meals. The owner Niko's very first question was whether Garfield was about to reappear on the island. Had they made it up? Were they together again? It was from Niko that Eden learned Garfield had not been here for at least two years. Then there were interminable questions about why she had not been back for so long, where she was living, if she was going to stay on the island. News was out among the local residents, foreign and Greek, that she had returned and an endless stream of old acquaintances and friends appeared at her table.

Eden recognised Sebastian walking across the port when he was still a good distance from her, on his arm a beautiful young woman with long blonde hair. Eden was aware of the way the girl clung to him, the passion they obviously had for each other. She was not at all disturbed by having been replaced so quickly in Sebastian's bed nor did she feel any sense of rejection.

On seeing Eden Sebastian went directly to her. Taking her by the hands, he raised her from her chair, enfolded her in his arms and kissed her. Then he introduced her to Janine. The young woman was obviously distressed at his attentions to someone else. Eden wanted to tell her, 'We've all been there one way or another with Sebastian so don't make the mistake of many before you and fall in love with him.' But she said nothing.

The following morning she knew how right she had been to keep her silence. Sebastian climbed the wall surrounding her property, entered through an open window and woke Eden with his lust for her. Neither of them mentioned Janine. During their erotic morning of sex and passion Eden found no time to think or feel emotional about rekindling a sex life with Sebastian. Their relationship had been too long dead and forgotten for her not to realise that at this time of her life she was aware of being two people: the woman of her youth, the brilliant cellist who emanated all things erotic, and the invisible middle-aged woman that time and life had changed her into.

At lunchtime Eden and Sebastian drank a bottle of champagne in bed leisurely, the winter sun streaming in at the window and warming their naked flesh. They touched and caressed each other and each retreated into their own thoughts. Eden's: that she must change, begin a new and different way of living. She must begin again, give up her old self to save herself. Once more Sebastian spoke as if he was reading her mind.

'You haven't asked me what I'm doing here,' he said.

'That's right, I haven't. What are you doing here, Sebastian?'

'Recovering from years of life and what it has done to me. I am setting aside years of solitude that never suited me, ego-driven successes that stole away the spontaneous joy I once lived by. Through all the shit that life threw at me, I was smart enough to have never given up the sexuality that has always been a driving force in my life. For that at least I am grateful.'

'You must be reading my mind, speaking the very thoughts and emotions occupying me. Sebastian, something, someone, is looking after me to have brought us together. You and I are both here weighing up the years of our lives and what they have done to us. Or, more to the point, what we have allowed them to do to us.'

With that she leaned across and kissed him passionately. First in gratitude, then in love for the path to freedom he'd laid before her, and then in lust.

For a long time after he'd left she stared out of the window at her beloved Hydra across the jumble of white houses and then out to sea, so blue and mysterious, romantic, very often looking up at Garfield's house. For a brief moment she imagined she loved him still. Once that moment had passed she understood that it was only the memory of loving him, of being loved by Garfield, that still lingered, nothing more. A tremor of emotion ran through her body. Was it someone walking over her grave? Garfield himself, his second wife, their son, Sebastian ... there once more trying to kick her back into life?

It had never occurred to Eden until her night of sex with Sebastian that until now, at this very moment, she had not recovered from her break-up with Garfield. When she had given up everything she had, everything she was, for him and there was nothing left to give, he'd walked out. His words rang in her ears now as if he were a ghost whispering from a corner of the room: 'You have too many problems. When you have sorted them and yourself out, I'll come back.'

She had loved him too much. All her youth and beauty, her talent, her money, were not enough. Had it been as simple as that? Yes, it had, if you stripped away the romance of love and lust.

Fame and fortune had been Eden's for most of her adult life. Except for the tragedy of losing her mother and father in a plane crash six months before she met Garfield, hers had been a charmed existence. But charmed lives do not prepare one for tragedy or bad times. Leila had had a will to live life to the fullest. It had made Teddy love her all the more, but was a lesson in life that Eden had found it difficult to live by once she was bereft.

Leila was piloting one of her lover's planes when she, her lover Randolf Herrere and Teddy were caught in a blizzard somewhere over the Rocky Mountains. After years of investigation the authorities were no closer to discovering the reason the plane went down. It had been hopelessly off course, that was all Eden had ever discovered about the accident. There had even been nasty rumours that the tragedy might have been more than an accident. A *ménage à trois* that went wrong. No one would ever know and once all the speculation died down Eden never wasted time on empty speculation. The loss of two fascinating and unusual people was all that occupied her mind.

As often as she could, on the anniversary of their death Eden returned to pay her love and respect to them by tossing flowers into the Aegean Sea off the island of Patmos where they had gone on their honeymoon after a grand wedding in Boston. They had always claimed that something quite spiritual had happened to them on that wedding journey that had bound them together for eternity and it was there that they wanted to return after death.

Eden at last turned away from the window and drew a bath for herself. Steeped in the hot water, she began to doze and time slipped away from her. Her thoughts drifted back to her second lover, Benjamin Gage. First Marshall then Ben. Who knows how her life might have turned out had they been different sorts of men? Not that she had any regrets about their being the men who'd formed her love and erotic life, then and for eternity. It was just a matter of curiosity and no more. Both of them were dead now any way, a part of her past, and nothing could change that.

Ben Gage had been a rebound from her loss of Marshall. As Eden sponged almond-scented water over her shoulders she realised that she had never really forgiven the men in her life who loved and finally walked away from her. How much of that had been her fault? Except for Marshall they had, every one of them, returned to claim her on her terms. Why then had she not been able to take them back? Timing. It had all been a matter of timing. They had shown their colours and were not there for her when she had most needed them. Their sin had been that they could not lay down their lives for her as she had done for them. It had been a matter of unconditional love. Would she have turned Marshall away as she had the others? Well, she would never know now.

Eden was dazzlingly young and beautiful with a talent so rare as to make her virtually unique when she met Ben Gage while on the rebound from her first love Marshall. The two men could not have been more different.

Ben Gage was fifty years old when she met him and they fell in love, a friend of her mother and father. He managed their investments along with several other friends of the Sidds. He was not particularly handsome nor did he have a great physique, but he had a marvellous

New England conservative charm about him, was kindness itself and had a sweet smile. He was irresistible to women. They adored his dependability and a certain sexiness in him that was evident no matter how subtle he was about it. He had always been well dressed, smooth around women and kind, a good pal to his men friends. He was that rare thing, a businessman with heart and compassion and a genuine love for art. Ben was happily married to an intelligent, sweet woman who ran a rather slapdash house of considerable size for him and their family. They lived on the outskirts of Boston and were socially prominent among the people he had grown up with. They frequented the music and art worlds and collected modern paintings, Rothkos and de Koonings, Marini sculptures and Henry Moores, when hardly a soul they knew was buying them.

Ben Gage adored his three sons, seemed outwardly content with his calm, peaceful existence and his attentions to his wife were envied by every woman in their circle of friends. But there was at the same time in him something quite secretive, a nurturing of secret desires he kept strictly to himself.

He had watched Eden grow up and both he and his wife Nora took her under their wing once she had lost Marshall. They and their children loved and admired Eden and were pleased when she gravitated towards them. Reviewing her time with him, Eden could hardly remember when she'd first realised she was deeply in love with Benjamin Gage, that she yearned to have an intimate life with him, that anything else was impossible to contemplate. What she loved most about Ben was the stable life he made for his family. Once she had become a part of his life and that family neither of them wanted to live without the other. Every time she went away on tour she fantasised that she could leave them, that she would be strong and give Ben up rather than demand a more intimate relationship. But passion, sexual desire, built up in her to such a pitch that on one occasion when Ben was driving her to the airport, she broke down and confessed her love and frustration at not having a sex life with him.

That first sexual encounter at the Copely Plaza was thrilling. The fear she had that they might be discovered added to the excitement of at last having sex with him. His passion for her, to feel him for the first time taking possession of her, remained still one of the highlights of her life. The control he showed in satisfying her sexual demands was frightening in itself. With exquisite care he devoured her body and soul. He wrung one orgasm after another out of her until she cried with the pain of pleasure on such a grand scale. Ben was an imaginative lover who introduced her to new sexual delights that she was able to enjoy because she trusted him implicitly.

That first night established a sex life for them that neither could live without. They added to each other's lives and, deceitful as it was, Eden made up her mind she would never allow their affair to infringe on Ben's life with Nora and the boys. She had never been happier. She had his family, his heart, a thrilling sex life with him. There came a time when he could not bear to be apart from her and so often she travelled with them on exotic holidays and always they found stolen moments to be alone together and have sex. They viewed the art galleries and collected paintings, dined in fabulous restaurants, the Gages attended her concerts, often flew to wherever she was playing merely for the evening. Ben and Eden's life was a series of sexual escapades and phone calls filled with erotic innuendo, conversations that left her warm and wet with lust for him.

Their sex life was conducted on the floor of his office, across his desk, over the back of an easy chair while his wife prepared dinner, in his car, hers, in a compartment on a train. They never could say no to each other and the fear of discovery only added to the excitement. It became obsessive for them, and then impossible for them to stop. They had been intimate for more than two years when one afternoon, after reducing each other to sexual oblivion in the bed Ben shared with his wife, Eden realised they could no longer go on. Their longing for a life together was too great. The deceit was beginning to grind into her soul. Eden was not yet twenty-one years old and debasing herself at every opportunity to have sex with Ben. It was not enough. She wanted more of him than she knew he could give her. She could deceive Nora no longer and knew she could never break up Ben's marriage, his home, lose him his place in staid New England society. That very night she told him, in floods of tears, that it had to be over for everyone's sake. She was leaving him to save herself and her dearest hope was that they could remain friends. He told her then that that was impossible for him, and so she lost the man she loved and his family.

Ten years passed. She tried to make contact with him several times but he would never take her calls. Then one day without warning he was announced by the doorman of her building in New York. Ben asked to see her. She refused but gave him her telephone number. He called and asked her to meet him for dinner in what had once been one of their favourite restaurants, El Parador. She agreed but arrived there with her current lover. As they all walked home together, Ben took her aside and told her, 'You are lovelier than ever. I still want you. Meet me tomorrow for lunch then we'll go shopping – Bergdorf, Saks, anywhere you want. I want to buy you something lovely. I told Nora about my love for you, that I was coming to get you. We can take it on from there.'

Jamie Worthing, her companion at the time, invited them in for after-dinner drinks. Ben never touched his, merely turned to Eden and said, 'You won't meet me tomorrow, will you? Come with me right now then and we'll forget the years that separated us.'

'It's too late,' was her only comment.

'Ten years too late, is that what you're saying?'

'I suffered too much during those years without a word from you,' Eden answered, a sadness in her voice that she remembered to this very day.

'I'm leaving,' he told her.

'I'll see you out,' offered Jamie from across the room.

'No, Jamie, I'll see Ben out,' Eden had replied.

At the door she asked him, 'Can we be friends?'
'No,' he had replied.
Six months later he was dead.

Chapter 6

The bath water was cold and that snapped Eden back into the present. She climbed out of the water, into a cream-coloured terry cloth robe, and went directly to bed. When she awakened it was dark outside and the telephone was ringing.

'You're settled in then?' were Max's first words.

'Yes, and delighted to be here.'

'There's an edge of happiness in your voice. An enthusiasm I've not heard for a very long time,' he told her.

'It's my attitude, dear Max. I have changed my way of thinking about myself and my life.'

'You no longer feel invisible?' he asked with genuine concern in his voice.

Eden laughed and proceeded to tell him, 'More a case of I'm through making myself invisible for others to ignore.'

'You've come a long way in a few days. It's grand to hear you speak of yourself this way.'

'Even now as we talk, I'm finding it impossible to

believe that I allowed myself to slide into being someone I never really was, only pretended to be. Max, you should have warned me that I was losing myself. Why didn't you?'

'Because I love you too much and accept you however you want to be.' His voice was soft with feeling.

They remained silent for several minutes. That same thing passed between them that had been lingering there for all the years they had been together. Whatever it was, neither of them seemed capable of labelling it 'love' or indeed felt strong enough to confront it as such.

Eventually it was Max who broke the silence. 'You've met someone!'

'A sometime lover, not a love affair, just someone who finds me erotically exciting and enjoys sex with me. Someone I never credited with being as wise as he is about me. Sebastian borders on indifference while at the same time enjoying me. It's as simple as that and just what I need to bring myself around to where I want to be. Does that sound like an easy rationalisation of a one-night stand with a promiscuous admirer?'

'It does rather,' replied Max with a note of disapproval in his voice.

Never willing to allow coldness between them, Eden asked, 'Forgive me.'

'There is nothing to forgive.'

'Don't be a hypocrite, dear Max. You always have to forgive me because I can't love you in the same way you love me. We know that pains us both.'

'One day our love for one another might change your

mind,' he told her as he had done hundreds of times before.

'Good night, Max. I kiss you,' was Eden's reply before she put the receiver down.

She sat in her darkened room, pressed her hands over her face and took long, deep breaths for several minutes, distancing herself from Max and her inability to love him the way he wanted her to, sexually and unconditionally.

Eden dressed and went down to the port to have her dinner. The Greeks adore living in the streets, detest being alone, and as a result one is never lonely in Greece. On Hydra there was no stigma attached to a foreign woman arriving alone for an evening out. She was merely swept up by any of the groups dining together who were always looking for more company to enjoy an evening with. A night out with friends, acquaintances and strangers was an evening well spent and nothing more. Social contact, fun or boring, never overlapped to the next day. It was a be here now society where all social barriers dissolved and joy in the immediate experience was all that mattered.

Eden was picked up immediately she entered the restaurant by such a group of Greeks who lived on Hydra and had several people in their party visiting from Athens. They knew who she was and showed their delight in seeing her after such a long absence from the island. Among them was Sebastian with yet another young beauty. He and Eden greeted each other affectionately but with some discretion which Eden was grateful for, although she was certain that the entire island was aware that he had made a recent conquest of her. It was the way several people raised an eyebrow and looked knowingly at each other that was the giveaway.

Always thinking about sex, Sebastian arranged the seating so that Eden was given a chair next to a young Greek man whom she had known merely to greet and no more in the past. Sotiri was handsome and sexy with an aura of erotic hunger about him. He was attractive, a well-known actor in the Greek theatre with enormous charm and a sharp wit. Eden was amused by him and unaware of his reputation as a lover of both men and women, a libertine who played sexual games with Sebastian as his accomplice.

Everyone knew of Sebastian's sex parties. Tales of them and his outrageous antics were gossiped about openly. It was as much a part of his life and theirs as breathing. Sebastian was discreet about the dark sexual side of his nature but never hid it.

The truth was that that sort of sex excited Eden as it did many women who had had brief sexual encounters with him but she had never been involved in one of Sebastian's orgies. Love, the desire to be loved and able to love in return on a grand scale, had always been a prerequisite for Eden before she would allow her own sexual wildness to surface from the depths of her being. That was why anything and everything was right sexually with first Marshall and then Ben, then best of all with Garfield.

At the table that night she picked up a sense of

overwhelming sexual excitement from both Sebastian and Sotiri that was difficult for her to ignore. She wanted them both and to be made love to by them at the same time. Erotic desire pulsed through her body, her fantasies took hold and the very thought of being dominated by their sexuality left her moist and limp with yearning for their sex in any form they were prepared to take her.

They went to her house after dinner, Eden escorted by the two men. She was unaware that Sebastian's young thing had been left behind at the restaurant until the three of them arrived at her gate.

'I think we've lost someone. Where's Frances?' asked Eden.

Sebastian took the key from her hand and opened the gate. 'This night is for you alone. Well, not quite. You and Sotiri and me.'

'Do I have any say in this?' she asked.

'None whatsoever,' answered Sotiri as he swept her off her feet and into his arms.

'From the moment you joined the table this night was cast for us,' Sebastian told her as he plucked her from Sotiri's arms and carried her into the house while kissing her.

Both men at the same time undressed and fondled her. It was difficult for Eden to tell where one began and the other left off. Once they had her naked two sets of mouths hungry for her licked and sucked on her flesh. She had come several times before they even had their clothes off. The two men exchanged places: one at her breasts sucking hard on her nipples, the other between her legs, taking her vaginal lips in his mouth and licking, devouring them as if they were soft, warm candy, his tongue lapping the ecstasy their acts had produced.

The sight of the men now naked and rampant, ready for their desire for sex unbound to take them over, made Eden's heart beat faster. They had magnificent bodies, this older man and this young Adonis of the theatre. They strutted their masculinity in front of her. Sebastian tied her hands by the wrists to the headboard of her bed and grazed her face with his penis, lowering his bollocks into her mouth. Her mouth thus filled, she rolled them around with her tongue, sucked on them while fondling Sotiri's hard and erect penis. Delirious with lust, lost to the real world, Eden was out in another dimension where sex and lust ruled. She was taken by her two lovers at the same time and then in turn and wept with that special kind of passion that comes when the self is dissolved in submission to all things erotic and out of the norm.

She had no idea when or how it happened but at some time she was released from her bondage and took over the two men. She drove them to the point of madness with her sexual aggression towards them only because it was fringed with adoration, a kind of love for a man and his body that is without violence or ego. Once in command of Sotiri she sensed that the young man had never had an encounter with anyone who took control of his sexuality as she did. It spurred her on to make demands of the two men she had never made before. To watch them, these two virile men, obeying her sexual commands of what they should do together was a new thrill for Eden. To see the men licking and sucking each other's hard phalluses quite shocked her and when they obeyed and penetrated each other on her orders her jealousy burst into rage and she stepped in and replaced each of them with herself. Heterosexual sex continued with a more intense lust than any of them had ever known.

In the morning Eden awakened wrapped in the arms of both men. It was not so much that she was shocked by the sexual thrills of the night before as that she found the entire experience so much out of her usual way of living. It was something that must have been lying dormant for years somewhere in her subconscious, this desire to be had by two men at the same time. She gazed at them, so handsome and peaceful in their sleep, left them and bathed in almond-scented water while reliving her night of lust. She had been to bed with two notorious libertines for the thrills that came with letting herself go, setting aside all barriers to convention. At heart she was a conventional woman, one who wanted to be as free as the men sleeping in her bed. But wanting doesn't make it so. One had to work hard to win such sexual freedom and the truth of the matter was that as much as she was prepared to do that, it simply was not enough for her. She wanted love to be a part of the equation. Another Marshall or a Ben or indeed a Garfield.

Sebastian and Sotiri in her bed had offered her much but with no strings attached. Delicious though she'd found that, it was hardly a replacement to the sort of lust and freedom she imagined with the right man, one who loved her passionately and loyally. That right man would automatically double her passion and settle her restless need to be loved. Was she looking for the impossible? No! For some strange reason that rebuttal stayed ringing in her head, clearer than any of the thoughts she'd had about love and relationships since the end of her life with Garfield.

It was true she wanted the thrill and the passion of the life she had had with him. She wanted to love as she had loved him, unconditionally, but this time with a good man, one who would love her in the same way. The very idea made her heart skip several beats. Was it too late to begin again in search of passion and love? Was she strong enough to do what she must to recapture the sort of life that satisfied her? These last ten years of retreat, had they been a necessary path to have taken so she might go forward on a last grand quest into life and what it still had to offer her?

Eden was contemplating these weighty questions while drinking a cup of coffee in front of the open fire in the kitchen. She was looking out on to the port and the choppy sea beyond when Sotiri walked into the room and poured himself a cup of the coffee. Neither of them said anything, merely looked at each other for several minutes before the actor spoke.

To Eden he looked more handsome than the night before, younger, even more sexual. A beautiful man in every sense of the word and with a glamorous masculinity about him that one rarely saw in young men these days. He was like a matinee idol of the forties and fifties in his looks and deportment and Eden could understand why he had such a huge following. She was dazzled by his maleness, the manner in which he looked upon her and held his counsel until he was ready to approach her. He understood without even knowing her that he was dealing with a proud and passionate artist, she could sense that in the gaze he directed at her across the table.

'You're more beautiful than I thought you to be last night when first we met,' he told her, speaking over the rim of his coffee cup and then sipping from it.

'I don't know what to say to that,' she answered, truly a bit flustered by the flattering remark.

'I did, of course, know who you were. When you were with Garfield I was envious of his hold on you. I used to stay in the background and watch you both. Once I even watched him fucking you on the rocks where you liked to swim. I fantasised that you would come to me one day and make love to me as you made love to him then. You never gave me a second glance.

'Last night was an erotic orgy of sublime sex. You were marvellous to have sex with. I could never have imagined that you would be so lustful, though. You were on fire with base sexuality when you took command of Sebastian and me. Neither of us had ever had each other and it will probably never happen again. We did it for you as well as for the sheer excitement of outrageous sex, for the thrills and moments of ecstasy for ourselves. I knew in my heart as I gave myself in to your demands that you would become jealous and enraged by what you saw. That's what I wanted because instinct told me I would then have you enslaved to me sexually, able to do anything I wanted with you. And I did. And now we have moved towards each other in a way that has bound us together for life. Neither of us will ever be able to forget last night. You, Sebastian and I went somewhere together that will have branded us forever. Tell me you understand and agree with me?'

'I don't know that I do. Last night was sexual madness that took me into a world of sex and lust, a night to remember, yes, but it was a small part of what makes up the whole Eden Sidd. Branded me for life? I think not, but only time will tell.'

'Last night you cast a spell on me. No woman, and I have had many, has ever submitted to me as you did and I certainly had never submitted to a woman so completely as I did to you. It was your passionate lustful nature that seduced me. I have never known such weakness and strength in one human being. It's voluptuous as is your creative genius. You have the world of human emotions in your hands and are, I sense, someone who knows how to spin it in your favour. I pray last night was only our beginning. You have captured my heart. Please don't break it.'

Eden was overwhelmed by Sotiri's beauty as a man, his erotic being as he confessed his feelings for her. She went to sit on his lap and stroke his hair. To kiss him gently on his cheek then on his lips. But she was lost for the words she needed to make him understand that she shared a sensuous feeling for him and nothing more. It had been sex on a mad, grand scale, nothing more. How to make him understand that and not hurt him at the same time?

He placed her hand on the hardness in his trousers. Eden unzipped them and, fondling him with her hands, slipped from his lap on to her knees before him and fed him slowly, lovingly, into her mouth, caressing him with its moist warmth and sucking him deep into her throat. Afterwards she rose slowly from the floor and left him sitting there in a lustful state.

Several minutes later Sotiri heard the glorious sound of the cello wafting through the house. She pulled at his heartstrings with her playing. Was it Bach, Beethoven, French court music of one of the kings of France? He had no idea. He only knew that she was playing it for him. She was telling him in the best way she could more of herself and what he should expect. It was not what he wanted to hear. He wanted her to confess all-consuming love for him. He wanted *her*, not a mere taste of her.

As youth and the arrogance of it took him over, he was certain that one day he would win her as his forever. She had seduced him as no other woman had ever done and he was convinced he could woo her to him as Garfield had done once. That she would grace his life with her love and passion. He would gain from her the will to fight on for the best life had to offer with no holds barred.

Sebastian entered the kitchen and saw the sexual state of his friend. He smiled and watched Sotiri fondling himself. 'You poor bastard,' was his only comment as he poured himself a cup of coffee.

With much difficulty Sotiri covered his passion for Eden and asked Sebastian, 'Why poor bastard?'

'Just listen to Eden playing – everything else in life comes second to her. It's always been that way with her. You haven't got a chance of anything more than what happened last night. Do yourself a favour and leave it at that. I've known her for years and I don't expect you will get a second taste of sexual madness from her.'

'You are forgetting her years with Garfield.'

'Don't tell me you're pitting yourself against him? You don't really think you can compete with their relationship.'

'I have youth and better looks on my side than Garfield ever had. I am as intelligent and as good at my work as he ever was at his. Eden is looking for passion and love and I am going to give them to her as he never did.'

'Don't be too sure of that. Eden loved him enough to give up heart, body and soul to him. Theirs was a love affair that happens once in a lifetime, if you're lucky. It burned them both out. You are more than fifteen years younger than Eden. She'll send you away to find a younger woman. She's no fool. It would be a mistake to think that she can't distinguish between love and sexual love. In that she is as much like a man as you or me.'

'I want her! I will have her! Will woo her until she is mine!'

'Good luck, you'll need it. I have seen her enslave a

man who loves her without even trying. His name is Max Kerwood and he has loved her for years. He's her agent and devoted suitor and that's what he will always be. They have been together professionally for more than twenty years and still, she hasn't given in to him. Unless she wants you as her true love, her Garfield, you haven't a chance to win her to you. The world is full of men who have wanted and missed capturing Eden for their own. She is a woman who picks and chooses who she wants. She has the innate belief, like most men, that she has the right to choose her own partner. We're not speaking here of some wallflower waiting to be plucked by Mr Right. My advice is to listen to her if you don't want to suffer in a one-sided love affair. She's a heartbreaker who doesn't even know it.'

The two men sat for some time listening to the music. Sebastian wanted to weep for the sheer beauty Eden was able to create. Sotiri sensed he was experiencing moments of greatness and knew he was out of his depth but an obsessive desire to possess Eden Sidd had already taken him over.

Aloud he said, 'She has genius, and what is genius but sustained passion? One day she will love me with that same sustained passion she has for her music.'

Eden was playing for both Sebastian and Sotiri. In gratitude or thanks for what she was not quite sure. A night of lust was certainly not the reason. Eden felt no need to do that and trivialise what had been an erotic frenzy shared equally by them all. The return of passion, then, of adventure to her life? That might be a possibility.

The confirmation of her being still a thrilling and attractive human being? It could even be that. Being plucked from the shadows of invisibility into the limelight where she'd dazzled and enjoyed herself as the Eden of her youth and beauty had done? Maybe so. Or possibly for all of those reasons she played, for them.

Eden felt herself bursting with confidence, a happiness with herself and what life had in store for her. The woman sitting in the Frog's Hollow tea room was barely recognisable now. A matter of a few days and the reality of her life was changing. She was grateful and full of wonder that she should have another chance. Her heart sang, soared to the stroke of her bow as it crossed the strings of her cello.

Chapter 7

In the days that followed Eden's night of sexual excess with Sebastian and Sotiri she walked the hills of Hydra, sat for long hours in the port drinking coffee or a glass of wine, and allowed a world she had once been prominent in to seep back in to her life. The community of foreign residents she had known for years were now older as she was. They still had the passion to live and let live on the island of their dreams, however. Behind the wrinkled faces youth and energy were still at work in most of them. They were an example to Eden of how not to give up and get on with living a full and enjoyable life. They had managed, as she had not, to combine solitude and fun and even in some cases careers – George Pender the painter, Leonard Cohen the singer-song-writer, several famous authors. They were living lives that were satisfying and where they were still making contributions to the arts and mankind.

Sotiri followed her around sniffing at her sexuality and she was flattered and succumbed to nights of his love and their debauchery. Each day she regained her strength as a woman and an artist and spent more hours playing her cello until she realised that she was practising with more determination and more creative flair with each hour that passed. Eden was making herself ready but for what she was not sure. Not until she called Max.

'I'm making a comeback,' she announced.

'Why am I not surprised?' was his reply.

'I don't know because I am. Will you put the wheels in motion?'

'How much time do you need to prepare yourself?'

'Six months should do it. And you to get us engagements?'

'I don't know off hand but I'll get on to it at once. This is thrilling! Your public has been waiting for this a very long time. We could kick off with a venue designed specifically for your return. You choose the place. It will be a sell out in the same way Pablo Cassals' return to playing in public was. That was in Puerto Rico and the world went there to hear and see him. You have no idea how long I have waited for you to make this call.'

The tenderness in his voice brought tears to her eyes. Max had loved her and her genius for so long and so faithfully. His support strengthened her now even though she hardly needed it. Her confidence had returned. It was then, at that moment, that she saw something else with startling clarity. Eden had never before understood that it was that devastating loss of confidence Garfield had inflicted on her that had driven her from the world's concert halls. She had always rationalised her retreat from the spotlight as stemming from exhaustion, a need to find herself, a desire to compose.

Eden Sidd's retreat of the last ten years ended one rainy lunchtime in the Frog's Hollow tea room in Tetbury. She was reincarnated in Hydra in the arms of two men.

Garfield Barton was sitting alone at a table in the Deux Magots reading the *International Herald Tribune*. It was one of those grey rainy days, cold and nasty for spring-time in Paris. But no matter the sheets of rain pounding on the empty tables and chairs outside, the puddles on the pavement and stream of water swiftly swirling down the street against the kerb, nothing could detract from the sight of the spring flowers: bright yellow daffodils, displays of hyacinths and tulips in stunning jewel-like colours, chestnut trees in full bloom. Garfield gazed through the plate-glass window on to the street. For several minutes he watched the chic Parisian women struggling against the weather under their silk umbrellas. Young and old alike were attractive to him. He was always on the look out for women whom he might enjoy and at the same time use to his own advantage.

He looked away from the view and caught the attention of the waiter with a click of his fingers to order a second espresso. This was part of his morning ritual: he'd wake up and his wife would bring them both a cup of morning tea and climb back into bed with him. They barely spoke to each other. Then Claudine would remove the empty cup from his hand and demand, with no great subtlety, her morning fuck from her husband. They had stopped making love years ago but the day was always that much sweeter for Garfield when he began it with morning sex. It was like adrenaline for him. She then drew his bath – something his first wife had never done – and he would bathe and dress. Claudine would vanish into her morning room where she would make calls. She was very social. Garfield would make his breakfast, walk to the Deux Magots having picked up a newspaper, spend the next hour or so in the cafe then walk to the Rue de Seine and enter the gallery at about midday. This would be his routine every day for the length of his exhibition at the Ramboulais Fils Gallery on the Rue de Seine. He almost never went to his studio to work when he was exhibiting.

Garfield had been a familiar face in the Parisian art world for twenty or more years so it was not unusual for artists, many of them famous, dealers and collectors to stop by his table for a gossip or a query as to how his exhibition was going. He had many acquaintances in the international art and music worlds, some he even considered friends. He was still passionate about all the arts and always looking for the opportunity to combine them with his own art form.

Garfield saw his creative persona as his entrée into high society. He had always thrived on being the artistic soul in the class that could afford to patronise art and artists.

He was handsome, a gigolo on a grand scale whose entire existence had always been bound up in furthering himself and no one else. He did it still with a charm, discretion, a pretence of humility, that never failed to enchant. His art was everything to him, his passion, his true love. Or so he led the world to believe. In fact there was nothing he would not do to further his own career, nothing he would not use, no one he would not manipulate, seduce, to get what he wanted or where he wanted to go. Garfield Barton was a natural born whore.

Early on in life, on his first trip to Europe the year he'd graduated from Yale, he'd met in Florence a struggling young painter, an Italian homosexual, clever and without a vestige of morals, not at all good-looking but with an abundance of old world charm. Dante Esposito was streetwise, an interesting painter, intensely ambitious. Just what Garfield most admired. They became partners in the struggle for fame and fortune in the art world, working the patrons and benefactors they targeted as a gay and straight friend struggling for their art and nothing else. They were good at it, the best. They charmed themselves into all the right circles and there they stayed, befriending the rich as well as the poor who crossed their paths, devious and clever in their drive to reap rich rewards wherever possible. Love never figured in their affairs, except possibly between the two of them.

Together they owned the house in Hydra that Garfield had received as part-settlement from the divorce with his first wife and a palazzo in Venice. That was where Dante was now as Garfield sat reading his paper in the Deux Magots.

He folded a page back. The first thing he saw was an

announcement of his own one man show. It was small, an inch by two inches, but Cecile Ramboulais had at least done what she had promised: a one man show, a dazzling vernissage, advertisements, a stunning brochure . . . and she had managed to sell five paintings. He was delighted. Those years of courting the sixty-five-year-old dealer had at last paid off for Dante and himself.

When it came to hustling the art world and both European and American high society, Garfield's having married a second time and fathered a son was no hindrance to him. If anything it added a certain gravitas to his image that he used adroitly to his advantage. Claudine turned out to be another Dante in Garfield's life. She, too, pimped for her man, and cared little about the way he lived so long as she remained Mrs Garfield Barton, and he loved and was good to their son.

Yes, life was very good for Garfield at the moment. Always a struggle but very good. Once more he turned the page of the newspaper and there it was: a quarter-page photograph of Eden. It quite took him aback. This was the first time he had come across her name in print in the last ten years. He almost never thought of her, so intent had he been on blocking her out of his life, out of his mind. His first reaction to seeing her face in newsprint was a flashback to having sex with her, how he could dominate her with it and the erotic world he drew her into. She had loved him beyond measure. He had left her because her love nearly ruined his life. Her success, her talent, her passion to live life to the fullest, her lust for him, had seduced him as he had never been seduced before. He had imagined her to be the well he could always draw from, that she would sustain him in everything without question and forever, that they were bound together as one and no one could break them asunder. That she would understand his and Dante's devious philosophy on how to live. Garfield had believed he could corrupt her into accepting their methods of winning and reaping their just rewards. She had, after all, managed her own path to fame and fortune.

He had always assumed she had done it by using every trick in the book as they had. Eden had fooled them both. Because of Garfield's years with her he nearly lost Dante as his ally and only true partner in life while the women he hustled resented his being with the beautiful cellist and he nearly lost their support too.

Garfield studied the photograph for several minutes, absorbed in it. Eden could still do that to him, even in newsprint, and he hated her for it. Bile rose in his mouth and he gagged on it, hating her the more as he remembered how she had fooled him. He had had a grand passion for her and she had cheated him. Had seduced him to believing she would lay down her life for him. And though she did in one sense, she had not in another; had failed to make him the star attraction she already was herself.

He closed his eyes to block her from his sight but that was even worse as his mind tantalised him with memories. The excitement of orgasm with Eden charged his body. Memories of sexual ecstasy, the power he'd had to make her come in floods of sweet excess, made him gasp.

Once more he snapped his fingers for the attention of the waiter and ordered a Pernod. He found his hand trembling as he added a long splash of water to the lime green liquid. As soon as it turned milky he drank from the glass. The bite of aniseed awakened his taste buds. He imagined the taste of Eden Sidd, so sweet and salty on his tongue. After reading the large print under the photograph Garfield tore the page from the newspaper, scrunched it into a messy ball and dropped it under the table where he kicked it sharply away from him with the toe of his shoe.

Garfield often thought of those great years when he had been with Eden – they were some of the best of his life. It had been Hydra, Paris, New York, a constant social whirl where all doors in the art world were held ajar for him and the woman on his arm. He never, however, thought about Eden as a human being in her own right, an artist with her own agenda, but rather blocked her out, pretended she had no real substance as Eden Sidd but only as a sensual, exciting, faceless woman who'd adored but ultimately cheated him, used him when he was so certain he was using her and could leave any time he chose.

A scene flashed through his mind: that fatal phone call, Dante calling from Venice. 'You must leave her today or all will be lost for us. The Contessa will make over her palace to her niece unless you come home and stay with her here. She longs for your love – and the sex, of course

– but she is growing impatient. Don't be stupid! You have allowed your cock to rule your head long enough. Eden Sidd may be a sexual delight but that's all she's been or will ever be. She's not one of us, just pretending to be. When it comes down to it, she hasn't the money or the courage to live as we do. She wants you all to herself. She's ruining you. You have forty-eight hours more left to play with her then, I warn you, it had better be over.'

Dante had of course been right about Eden. Garfield had owed her no explanation and when he walked out on her never gave her one. She'd had her problems: the tragic death of her mother and father had been an enormous loss to her, plus financial worries and a career she had been distracted from when love had moved in on her. Yes, he had had the best of Eden and now there was nothing left. The well had run dry. It was over. Time to move on. He never gave it a second thought and was gone within twenty-four hours of Dante's phone call.

Garfield paid his bill. After turning his collar up against the wind and the rain, he walked swiftly from the cafe through the flooded streets to the gallery. He was drenched through to the skin by the time he entered it. There was no one there except Cecile and her assistant. She took Garfield to her flat above where she towel dried his hair, cared for and attended to him as he remembered bitterly that Eden had never made such loving gestures towards him. That was, of course, not true, merely a selfish stretch of the imagination so that he might dislike her that little bit more. Hold her in contempt of his heart.

Cecile kissed him on the cheek, then his lips. She removed his wet jacket and shirt and, drying him off with a fresh warm towel, she caressed his chest and kissed his nipples. He gazed deeply into her face, so well cared for for a woman her age. But her eyes gave her away. They were old eyes, dimmed by age, hardened equally by success and disappointment. He knew what she wanted, what price he must pay for her devotion to his work, her passion to keep him as friend-painter-lover. He unzipped his trousers and turned her over the back of the easy chair, plunging into her forcefully. He fucked her deeply, roughly. She begged him to slow down, he was hurting her, but he placed a hand over her mouth and continued. He felt her give in to her orgasms. They came repeatedly and swiftly and Cecile was lost in ecstasy, moving to the rhythm of his every thrust.

Garfield was lost in the acts of hatred and sex. In his mind he was having sex with Eden, dissolving her into a puddle of need for him to fuck her to death, which in fact was almost how it had been between them. He could not, did not want to, stop. He continued for a considerable time before he came into Cecile with a powerful orgasm. Release sent him collapsing to the floor still holding on to Cecile who was crying: from fright, pleasure, pain and gratitude.

They were both gasping for breath. Tears were brimming in Cecile's eyes. She loved him. That she could inspire such passion in Garfield inflated her ego. He was hers, this younger man, still so handsome and virile. He could have any woman he wanted but enjoyed her beyond all the others. She knew that he was a hustler of women and what the price was to have him as a lover. She paid it, not too gladly, but paid it nevertheless. It was his love and adoration of her and fucking such as they had just had together that made it all worthwhile.

Cecile needed to bathe and change her smart little black dress. The violence of Garfield's sexual assault had left her bruised, quite undone. When she returned to the sitting room where they had had their tryst, she found him sound asleep on the carpet in front of the open fire, naked, his thumb in his mouth, looking like an innocent child. Cecile's heart pounded. Her mouth went dry. She loved him too much. No matter how much she deluded herself, she knew that to be a fact but she could live with it. She covered him with a cashmere blanket, stroked his hair, caressed his cheek and left her flat.

Laurent Touvier had not seen Eden Sidd for more than a decade when Max Kerwood approached him. The two men met in Paris at the Le Grand Vefours for lunch on that same rainy cold spring day. It was by no means an awkward meeting. They had always been great friends, accepting their respective roles in Eden's life. If anything they had missed each other's company during the parting of the ways after Eden had rejected Laurent's offer of marriage and run off with Garfield.

They embraced each other and were ushered directly to their table. Max was amused by the number of people who rose from their chairs to shake Laurent's hand and introduce him to the other guests at their table. Max walked ahead, smiling at this show of success and popularity, remembering when Laurent had been an unknown, a protégé of Leonard Bernstein's.

Laurent had not disappointed Max. When the two men first met fifteen years before Max had earmarked him as potentially one of the greatest conductors of the twentieth century. He had not been disappointed. Every year that passed was proving Max to have been right as Laurent stunned the concert halls and opera houses of the world with his genius.

Max watched him from the banquette where he sat. Still so young-looking at forty-five, and handsome, so virile yet sensitive in his looks and deeds. A little more arrogant, possibly, but that was no bad thing. A form of self-protection?

Laurent sat down opposite Max and was offered a glass of champagne by the waiter. He raised his glass and gave the toast: 'Eden.' He said no more but pressed his lips to the rim of the flute and drank.

The two men studied the menu and made their selections; afterwards Max ordered the wines from the sommelier. They were a grand white for the first course, a Montrachet, with a noble Pétrus afterwards to go with their beef.

'You're being very generous, Max. You are either terribly pleased to see me and this is a celebration or else you want a very great favour,' quipped Laurent.

'Both,' Max answered him with a smile.

'Now we have that out of the way, tell me, how is Eden?

'She's well. Better than she has been in a long time, in fact.'

'She never married?' asked Laurent.

'No. And you haven't, I know. Still too taken up with long-legged beauties, glamorous young things hopeful for an offer of a wedding band. Isn't that the scenario?'

Laurent gave Max a knowing smile and answered teasingly, 'I am an agent's delight, Max. My work is my life, public and private. All the rest is just public relations. I have on occasion come across Garfield incidentally.'

'He's been out of Eden's life for more than a decade.'

'I loved her. You will never know what it cost me when she turned me down to run off with him. But why talk about that now?'

'You still love her!' said Max with genuine surprise in his voice.

'I don't think much about love or Eden. If you don't mind, subject closed,' Laurent replied.

'I'm afraid it's not,' said Max ruefully.

They exchanged glances across the table that revealed more than either of them could possibly have wanted. They were two men in love with the same woman and most probably for the same reasons, one who had ultimately rejected them. Brothers under the skin.

'You're here about Eden. I should have guessed.'

'Laurent, I'm organising a comeback concert for her. She would like you and the Boston Symphony Orchestra to be a part of her first appearance in ten years.'

'It's a long time to be silent in the music world,' was Laurent's cautious reply.

'And if I were to tell you she's as good now as she was at her peak, would you have another answer for me?'

'I would have to hear her myself to see if she is as good as you say. Then we might have something to talk about.' Laurent quickly added, 'I said *might*, Max. I make no promises, is that clear?'

Max sat back in his chair, more relaxed about this meeting than he had expected to be. Laurent Touvier, one of the brightest and most exciting of the present-day classical conductors, had not said no.

When Eden had suggested that she wanted to come back with Dvorak's Cello Concerto, Richard Strauss's 'Don Quixote' and Lalo's Cello Concerto in D Minor, with Laurent conducting the Boston Symphony Orchestra and the venue the amphitheatre at Epidaurus, he had known that the most difficult thing would be getting Laurent to agree.

Max was all too aware how deeply hurt Laurent had been when Eden had refused to become his wife. The age difference of ten years had been her excuse. He was younger than her with a career still to establish. It was what he had not as yet experienced that was keeping them apart, she maintained. Then Garfield walked into their lives and swept Eden away from Laurent. The way Eden looked at Garfield, that passionate love that swelled between them, was something Laurent had wanted to experience with her but it had never happened, even

Max had seen that. Oh, something had happened, a sensual and emotional coupling, but it had never been all-consuming for Eden as it had been for Laurent and still was for Max.

He looked up now from his plate of *foie gras* and sipped from a glass of Sauternes. 'You never thought you could forgive her for not loving you the way she did Garfield,' he told Laurent. 'You wore your heart on your sleeve and did not go down with dignity. You let the world know how much you had loved her, that she had toyed with your emotions and walked away into another man's arms. But at the same time you acknowledged that Eden had done a great deal for your emergent career, how much you had learned from her, that your life was enhanced by the years you had been together, that you owed her everything. Think about that and leave it firmly in the past. She is a different woman nowadays and you a different man. She needs you, wants you for this return and maybe for love.'

Max, on mentioning Eden's need for Laurent to love her, realised he had hit on something he had not fully considered before. In truth, having tossed Laurent away in the heat of her passion for Garfield, Eden had lost out on what should have been the love affair of her life. It most probably would have given her a lasting relationship and all she had missed: a husband, family, devotion from someone on equal terms with genius as herself, and not least success.

In fact all the things Max had wanted to give Eden himself but could not because she didn't want them from him any more than she had wanted them from Laurent. That was the tragedy of Max's life as it had undoubtedly been of Laurent's as well.

So many things clicked into place as he sat opposite Eden's former lover eating lunch. She had wanted those things from Garfield and her tragedy was that he could not and would not give them to her. It had taken her unhappy affair with him and her years of semi-seclusion afterwards to make Max understand how right he was about Eden's really needing and wanting Laurent. He suddenly felt guilty for never having faced that truth and helping her to see it for herself. Selfishness, pure selfishness, because as long as she made no life with another man, she was his. But something in his heart told him that this time around Eden would be wiser with Laurent. Her experience of loving Garfield and her retreat of these last ten years would have matured her. This time she would recognise what she'd had and could have again with Laurent.

Max was somewhat traumatised by these revelations, but he loved her very much and wanted her to be happy and back on the world stage so he took a deep breath and remained strong, continuing with his lunch and trying to convince Laurent to meet Eden.

'She's giving you a second chance to become a part of her life. This return is no small thing for her. She chose you of all the conductors of the world who adore her as an artist and would be willing to work with her.'

'Stop pushing so hard, Max. Where is she staying? At the Crillon?'

'No. She's not in Paris. She's been in Alexandria for the last six weeks.'

Laurent felt a rush of excitement course through his body. The villa in Alexandria was one of Eden's favourite retreats. Its owner was Magdi Sharif, an admirer with whom she had once had an affair. Laurent had met him when he himself spent a glorious week at the villa with Eden, Magdi, and Magdi's glamorous and sophisticated friends in a house party that still remained one of Laurent's most cherished memories.

'The villa on the sea?' he asked, his voice softer as was the look in his eyes.

'Yes, Magdi's villa. She's always worked well there. No chance of any hassle from the music press about this momentous return.'

'Let's talk dates. My schedule is already set for the next two years. We would have to do it during one of my holiday breaks.'

'Then you'll do it?' exclaimed a delighted Max.

'I didn't say that, Max. We'll take this step by step. First let's see if we can come up with a date, then I have to meet Eden and she must play for me. As it happens I have a break for the next three days. Get her here by then and arrange a meeting.'

'You'll have to go to her in Alexandria. That's where she wants to meet you. I'll arrange everything.'

'I don't think Eden is in a position to make demands,' said Laurent, a hint of peevishness in his voice.

'When has that made any difference to her when she wants something? Trust me, she's not playing a power game here. If she wants you in Alexandria, you can be sure that is the best place for you two to meet.'

'She will not turn my life upside down again, I will not allow it,' Laurent warned. He excused himself then and left the table.

Chapter 8

Laurent had only three days and four nights before his next engagement at the Paris Opera House for Rameau's *The Loves of the Indies*. It was to be a star-spangled production and he was ready for it. All the French opera world was anticipating its exploding volcano special effects and the extensive use of ballet dancers in a long and difficult opera that was rarely performed.

One more rehearsal would have been more advantageous to Laurent than running off to Egypt to confront Eden. And why do it anyway? He tried to rationalise his decision: because she needed him, because if she was still as great a cellist as she had been he wanted no other conductor to share her return. It belonged to him. The truth was that there had never been and would never be anyone in his life like Eden Sidd. He was still in love with her.

Laurent had never had the chance to confront Eden and hopefully reach a closure that would set him free from her at last. He fantasised that she would look old and have lost her sensuality, that easy charm she had always exerted over men. That the golden charisma of Eden Sidd would have turned to dross.

Yet here he was on a chartered twelve-seater Gulf Stream, jetting across Italy towards the coast of Egypt courtesy of Magdi Sharif's generosity. Laurent looked across the empty seats to Max before he dozed off.

The day was slipping away, an orange sun hanging against a dusky sky, when Max awakened him. The plane had landed and they were ready to disembark. The heat was not overpowering but it was decidedly close and humid. Laurent stepped from the plane on to the tarmac. He was feeling dizzy, not quite awake and yet very much so. Emotionally on edge. Seated in the rear seat of the Rolls-Royce that had awaited their arrival, Laurent realised he was excited to be once more in Alexandria. It had once been for him a romantic and mysterious city, sensual, lustful. Now that he was back he sensed a pulsating excitement that had been missing from his life for a very long time.

Magdi's Mr Fixit took their passports and had them stamped at the gatehouse where they exited from the airfield. They sped away towards the centre of the city. The scent of Alexandria hung in the air: salt air from the sea; jasmine blossoms strung into necklaces and sold by vendors running along the roadside to catch romantic drivers; garlic from pots of frying chickpeas, and lamb and goat's meat roasting over charcoal; ripe and over-ripe fruit sold off carts being pushed along in the traffic. Above all these the scent of sand and dust seeped into the car and stirred memories for both men.

The sunset was long, slow and luscious as the car threaded its way among the carts pulled by men, donkeys bearing loads, scooters honking their horns, dilapidated lorries and smart cars, and what seemed like thousands of men, some in western dress but mostly in long robes and wearing turbans on their heads. The sight of Egyptians, the sweetest of all the Arabs, moving through the streets as if in slow motion made Laurent feel close to the earth and mankind.

They crossed the city towards Marsa Matruch and the desert. Here the populace thinned out to a trickle of people. Once more he saw grand houses, mini-palaces that faced the sea behind high walls, closed gates and guards, luscious palm groves, stunning gardens. Magdi's villa was one of them. Built at the turn of the nineteenth century by a famous French architect, it was huge, elegant, grand and strange all at the same time. Strange for the fact that it seemed to be isolated in another era: the years of opulence when Farouk ruled as King and the French and English incomers thronged to cosmopolitan Cairo and Alexandria. There was besides something amazingly romantic about the palace that Magdi chose to call a villa and its setting. Sections of it were constantly crumbling and being washed away by high tides and strong waves. Magdi seemed sublimely unconcerned.

When the Rolls drew up to the entrance to the house a stream of servants emerged to greet Max and Laurent. They had obviously expected Magdi to be with the new arrivals but the Major Domo took charge in his place,

.arranging for their luggage to be sent to their rooms. He dispersed most of the staff and was about to usher Max and Laurent into the house when they heard music. Max placed a hand on the Major Domo's arm and instructed him, 'Henri, take us to Madame Sidd.'

Rather than go through the house, Henri Piquet led the two men through the garden, up one terrace and down another, past a swimming pool perched on a rock formation overlooking the long deserted beach and undulating aquamarine waves. They were drawn by the passionate sound of the cello, vibrant and compelling. Laurent was immediately overwhelmed by Eden's mastery of her instrument. The years rolled back for him and he was once again young and untried. Then their passion for and dedication to music was something they shared and brought them to love. He wanted to weep with joy to be in her presence again and to hear her pouring her heart and the heat of her lust for life into her playing. He could think of nothing but seeing her again, bathing in her light.

Impatient now actually to see her, he turned to Max and the Major Domo and asked, 'Where is she?'

Henri led them through a double-height conservatory with many broken panes of glass and a veritable jungle of exotic plants and trees. Orchids bloomed prolifically on branches. The warm sea breeze drifted in and stirred their blossoms. The scent of honeysuckle and jasmine filled the air. The men walked through the remains of the once magnificent glass house on floors of black and white marble mosaic. Laurent was enchanted once again to see the orchid house, finding it even more exotic and romantic a ruin than he had remembered. Ten years of salt air and neglect had only added to its rare beauty. The music grew louder. He was coming closer to Eden.

Laurent's first sight of her was from the white sand of the beach. He and Max had walked down to it through the orchid house's missing wall and on to a terrace where they were forced to hop over a crumbling balustrade. The jewel-like blue-green of the waves rushed towards their feet, making them walk briskly towards the music. Then they saw her silhouetted against the backdrop of the gazebo, its Doric columns and domed roof stark against the endless sky. The sun slipping slowly towards the horizon cast a fiery light on Eden: a lonely figure barefoot upon the warm sand covering the folly's floor. She was dressed in white gossamer, so fine that its hem rippled from the warm, sweet breeze and every stroke of her bow. Her eyes were closed. Eden was lost in her music and even more delectable than the last time Laurent had seen her.

Max was scrambling up a sand dune to reach her when Laurent caught up with him. 'I should prefer to conduct this reunion without an audience. Will you grant me that?'

Max had little choice but to say yes, though something in his heart broke then. Once more he would sacrifice his deeper feelings for Eden so that she might find love with someone else. As he stood by and saw her one-time lover eagerly approach her he told himself he would have to be very strong because these two passionate souls would inevitably find each other again.

Laurent moved as quietly as a panther on the prowl after his quarry. When he stepped into the gazebo he leaned against one of the crumbling columns and listened for some time before Eden opened her eyes, saw him and stopped playing. She didn't move from her chair, simply looked across at him. They gazed into each other's eyes.

After several minutes of silence except for the sound of the waves rolling on to the beach it was Eden who spoke. 'I can hardly believe you are here, just listening to me play. I know what it must have taken for you to come to my aid. I'm grateful.'

A gracious greeting, thought Laurent, his heart racing. He loved her still. She did not look a day older than she had on that horrible morning when she'd walked away from him. He wanted to hate her. Fantasised that he could walk up to her now and say how badly she had played. That he had only come to audition her and tell her he would not conduct for her already publicised return to the concert platform. His head was swimming with horrible things he wanted to say to hurt her. His silence, his inability to lie to her, spoke volumes to them both.

Without uttering a word he walked over to her. He took her hand in his and she rose slowly from her chair. Laurent took her cello from her and placed it and the bow carefully in its case. Then he clasped her in his arms and held her, pressing her hard against him. His first words to her were, 'It will be one of the finest concerts to be heard in this century. Welcome home.'

'Then you will conduct the orchestra?'

'Yes,' he answered.

Eden reached up to ruffle his hair then stepped back into his arms. It was she who kissed him first. The warmth of her lips, the sensuality of that kiss, took him off guard. He gave in to the embrace and slipped slowly into a place where he felt warmed to the core of his being. The place where he had once dwelt before Eden walked away from him. Older and wiser now he understood that she was giving him everything she could at that moment. That she was sincere, that she loved him now as much as she was capable of loving any man. Could she, would she, sustain this moment of love for him? Questions were whirling round his head. He hushed them with a resolution to this time round take his love for Eden a day at a time.

She stepped away from their kiss in full awareness of the love and lust ignited by it. She found Laurent more attractive if anything, liking the stamp of success he now had about him: a certain arrogance in his step, the way he held his head. He had earned the right, she thought. She had not taken it for granted that he would work with her and felt humbled that he did not hesitate or play games with her about doing so. A lesser man might have.

Eden sighed. Reaching for her cello with one hand, she took Laurent's hand in the other. Together they walked from the gazebo and down a dune to the beach. Taking the case from her hand, he carried it for her. She stopped and bent down and removed his shoes and socks, called out to one of the house servants who was walking towards them and gave him the cello to take back to the house.

'Let's walk along the shore for a bit,' she suggested.

The waves washed over their feet as with arms linked they walked along the beach. 'Are you married? In love? Is there someone special in your life?' asked Eden.

'Not married, not in love, there is no one special in my life,' he lied. It was a lie because as he'd discovered the moment he met Max for lunch only the day before, he was still in love with Eden and she would always be the special woman in his life.

The water swirling round their ankles was warm and inviting. Eden bent down and scooped some into her hands, splashing it over her face and shoulders. Then, looking happy and many years younger than her age, she waded into the water up to her waist. The white gossamer of her dress floated free around her. Laurent followed her in after peeling off his linen jacket and shirt. He stepped from his trousers and left them in a heap. When he was standing next to her, hand in hand, they waded out into deeper water.

There was an air of eternal youth about Eden that captivated him. It was there in her laughter, in her eyes, in the way she'd played. Laurent found it difficult to look away from her. It was Eden who broke from him to swim further out in the shallow water. Laurent did not follow but struck out in another direction. Later they did meet up and playfully splashed about for several minutes before, hand in hand, they walked from the sea.

Eden was naked under her dress. The wet, white gossamer cloth clung to her body, one Laurent had loved and indulged himself in, one he wanted now. He could not hold back but went to stand before her. He ran his fingers through her wet hair and smoothed it away from her face, then he caressed her breasts, pinched her erect nipples and raised the hem of her skirt so that the soft hot breeze might dry her dress and hide her lusty body. Almost immediately the material went opaque. A sensual tension was developing between them and had to be set aside. That was not what they were about, at least not for the moment. They had hardly spoken to each other and there was much to be said between them.

Eden reached out to him and slid his wet shorts off him. She held out his trousers for him, dressing him lovingly rather than erotically. Once he was dressed and the heat of the late afternoon had dried out her dress, they clasped hands and headed back to Magdi's villa. Finally they began to talk.

'I never stopped thinking about you,' Laurent told her.

'Not always lovingly, I'm sure, and you would have been right,' she replied.

'It hurt too much, your dismissing me like that. Falling in love with Garfield.'

'I know. It couldn't be helped, Laurent. If I could have spared you that hurt, I would have. Garfield was a grand passion. You have to understand that I have no regrets about my affair with him. I am just lucky that I survived it. It taught me what love is not, opened my eyes to what it can be.'

'What has prompted this return to the concert hall?'

They were mounting the steps to the terrace of Magdi's house when she pulled him down to sit next to her. She heard the rustling of a man's robe and called out in French, 'Youseff, drinks, please. Champagne.' Then turning back to Laurent she told him, 'You're very handsome, still as attractive to me as you have always been. Women must chase you.'

Eden was flirting with him and much as he wanted her, this time round he had every intention of seeing to it that neither of them would be hurt. Though he sensed it might indeed be satisfying to hurt her. Sweet revenge could be easily slipped into.

Chapter 9

'You were about to tell me why you have returned to music?' Laurent reminded her.

'So I was,' she replied.

He saw her hesitation. This was clearly not the reunion she had anticipated. What had she expected? That he would sweep her off her feet into bed, rekindle the fire that had once burned so bright as it fed on their lust for each other? Well, this time she must win and cherish his passion for her, he vowed.

'I never really left music, Laurent, just performing in public. I did play every day, am proud of the pieces I have composed during those years. I have had a good life off the concert circuit but if truth be told a better one on it. I realised that one day in a tea room called Frog's Hollow.'

Then Eden told the story of how she'd realised she had become invisible. Just another statistic: middle-aged, fading female who could no longer turn a man's head.

Tears filled her eyes but the power of her will held them back from cascading down her cheeks. Her voice remained firm and she was quite magnificent when she told Laurent, 'I simply could not allow myself to be thrown on to the scrap heap. I left immediately on a journey to find myself again. To seek that happiness, the joy in life, I used to have and which attracted men to me. I wanted them to see me again as someone alive to loving and being cherished.

'At the start of my odyssey, I thought I had only to find a man to love me. It was a humiliating thing to put myself through and, thank the lord, I realised almost immediately that it was me, Eden, who had to fall in love with myself again, not some stranger or old friend just because he had a penis to entice me with. That I needed to work on myself as I always had. No one looked at me as a vital passionate woman any more because I had somehow managed to let that side of my life die. The moment I reached down and found the Eden I had been before my retreat, I was no longer invisible to men.

'It took two of them in Hydra to restore my sexuality to me. Afterwards I found that to search for a man to love me, to seek out men who wanted me for sex and lust alone, was fun again but too shallow a goal. Every day I would practise and every day I sensed I was playing the game better. Every night I was made love to my sensuality was restored, my very soul.

'That was no little thing. To desire on a grand scale again is like a rebirth. To go out on the edge of sexuality for the excitement it can bring is comparable with nothing else. How had I forgotten that? How could I have deprived myself of that luxury? I was invisible to that handsome stranger because I'd allowed my passion to die, had become a shell of the woman I once was.

'Working on my music every day, I was aware that there was almost immediately a change in my playing. It happened incredibly fast, so fast I wasn't at first sure that the gift I have been endowed with, my ability to play the cello, was still there. If it had not been I would never return to playing in public. But I feel now that my return is almost preordained. It is my destiny to play again.'

Here Eden stopped. She had not meant to blurt out the incident at Frog's Hollow to Laurent of all people. This younger man whose love she had abused, whom she had hurt so badly if unintentionally. 'I'm sorry, I didn't mean to go on so. I must sound vain, frivolous, desperate even. But you did ask, and that's what happened.'

That was so typical of Eden, to tell it as it was. No cover up. No flattering story to ingratiate herself with him. Now he had to assimilate the fact that she was enjoying a sex life with other men and had called on him not to rekindle a lustful relationship but a musical one. He sat for several minutes. They were silent, sipping from their champagne flutes and gazing into each other's eyes. How lovely Eden looked, lovely and sexy and exciting, just as she had always been for him. The sexual chemistry was still there. It excited them, that was evident, but what to do about it was not.

'Sorry?' he said. 'You do not have to be sorry for confiding in me. If you had talked to me as you just have, truthfully and from the heart, all those years ago when we were together, our love might have blossomed instead of died. That is all I ever want to say to you about our love that went wrong. You are playing wonderfully. I *will* conduct for you. We can deal with that. Whether we can with you and me together in an intimate relationship again is a question that only our being together and time can answer. Just assure me of one thing: if we should rekindle our intimate relationship it will not be purely because you want me to conduct for you, will it? That we can keep work and our private feelings separate, if there are to be any.'

Eden was taken off guard by the generosity that Laurent was exhibiting. That he was here at all and willing to conduct for her was marvellous good luck but to have such a mature attitude about them, that he even considered that there still was a them, was an extra bonus she had not even considered. This time round it was only fair that he should make the moves towards any intimacy and she must be cautious in every way not to lead him on as she had once done.

Eden rose from the step and Laurent followed. She handed her empty glass to him and, sliding her arms around his waist, leaned in against him. 'Would you prefer me to choose another conductor?' she asked.

'No.'

'You are sure about that?'

'Yes, quite sure. The concert first. Love and attachment, if they are to be our destiny, will have to wait.'

★ ★ ★

Laurent and Eden went to their respective rooms where they bathed and changed for dinner. Max was in the drawing room when Laurent appeared. The two men shook hands which instantly seemed strange to both of them. They laughed about it, grateful that the gesture took the edge off the awkwardness that had developed between them for a minute. The laughter reminded each of them that any awkwardness at this stage of their relationship was unnecessary, even ridiculous.

'I think the first thing to settle on is the date of the concert,' suggested Laurent as he pulled a slim Hermès diary from the inside pocket of his jacket.

The two men discussed possible dates for Max to work on. There was not only Laurent to consider but the availability of an orchestra and the amphitheatre to be booked. They arrived at three possibilities and a decision to hold two concerts on consecutive nights. Max could sense Laurent's professional excitement about Eden's return.

Diaries set aside he enquired, 'How did you find her?'

Laurent thought the question a natural one but loaded. He replied, 'Magnificent, Max. You know, in the past Eden was always modest about her own achievements. I think she owes it to herself to leave modesty behind at this stage of her career. Her artistry is tied to her personality to an extent that makes her personally vulnerable, but so what? She's a strong lady. She has accomplished much in the past but nothing to what I feel she can and will do now. I'm thrilled to be aboard for this ride.'

Max wished that he had been there for the epoch-making reunion between these two great artists. He would like to have known how intimate a relationship Laurent and Eden were going to have as well. But Laurent was right about Eden's attitude: the modesty and secrecy about her private life that she had always insisted upon would have to go. The public relations campaign would have to be clever and relentless to bring her back in grand style for all the world to acknowledge.

The men were talking about Epidaurus when Eden joined them. They stood up to greet her and immediately sensed the sensual aura that entered the room with her. Momentarily these two men in love were struck dumb. What after all did Epidaurus matter in the wake of their obsessive love for Eden? A love and adoration, a respect, that no other woman could engender in them.

In a long black linen dress, its halter neckline plunging provocatively in the front and bare-backed to the waist, Eden looked every inch the elegant lady with her hair pulled back and dressed in a French twist. On her ears were a pair of large square-cut emeralds surrounded by diamonds. Laurent remembered them as having been her mother's.

Leila was still a legend in the music world for her beauty, charm, love for and patronage of music, and for Laurent special because she had been the first person to champion him when he was still a boy. He, like everyone else who ever met Leila Sidd, had been dazzled and later enchanted by her. For the first time now, seeing Eden enter the room, Laurent understood how similar she was to her mother, only more special because she had an incomparable artistry that Leila never possessed. He was quite shaken by her entrance and the prospect of once again being part of her life.

Both men gallantly greeted her with a kiss on her hand. They were in the large drawing room overlooking the sea. It was still very warm and humid and the sound of the waves breaking against sections of the house gave an air of excitement and adventure to the room with its half-dozen arched twenty-foot-high windows draped in sheer muslin and apricot silk taffeta.

The room itself was sensual, exotic and beautiful. Oriental carpets covered most of the parquet floor and the furniture was sleek and elegant French of the Directoire period. On the many side tables silk-shaded lamps and Chinese vases of the Ming, Tang and Han Dynasties were lit to give the room its soft warm glow. Chaise-longues were draped with silk embroidered shawls, settees wood-trimmed and covered in tattered brocades. Books in old leather bindings were piled high on marble tables. Many orchid plants in full bloom were dispersed between the potted palms. Gazing down upon the guests from the walls were family portraits of dusky beauties who had ruled the house through the ages, handsome men in robes and turbans who had left their mark on the house and their country, for the Sharifs had always been foremost in advising the Kings of Egypt. But that was in another time, long gone but not forgotten. History and this room could attest to that.

'I had forgotten how marvellous this house is. This

room conjures up such memories. Will Magdi be joining us?' asked Laurent.

'No,' answered Eden. 'He is with the President of Egypt at a meeting at the UN.'

'Good memories, I hope?' said Max.

'The best. I was actually quite shocked on my first visit, thought the house party depraved and decadent. To begin with anyway. I was so young and innocent then.'

'Are you suggesting that I corrupted you?' asked Eden teasingly.

'Certainly not. Dazzled me perhaps. I left here enchanted, grateful that my week here with you and Magdi and the house party had opened my eyes to how much fun one can have when the barriers are down and sex and love, passion and lust, take over. I had never known life could be so frivolous. I will always be indebted to Magdi and you, Eden, because when it was good it was great.'

'But when it was bad it was horrid!' she said and the moment she'd spoken was sorry.

'That was the problem. It was never bad, just abruptly over. But that was the past and it's over with. I did say we should let it rest in peace. We're not here to go over old hurts.' He immediately changed the subject. 'Why Epidaurus, Eden?'

'Because the theatre in there is the most famous and best preserved of antiquity. Have you not seen it?'

'Yes, I have. I once saw a performance of *Medea* there. It was overwhelmingly impressive.'

'Precisely!' offered Max. 'And a remote location that only real music lovers will want to go to to hear Eden's return performance.'

Laurent ignored Max's answer and approached Eden about it once more. 'That really doesn't tell me why you chose it. Can it only be because of its antiquity?'

'Not wholly the reason but partly so. I adore Epidaurus. That is probably the main reason. It was an emotional decision, that's for sure. There's something very inspiring for me about it every time I visit, usually every few years. That perfect bowl stone shape rising up the hill surrounded by twisted old trees. And the acoustics are remarkable. Whenever I make a visit I sit in the sun on the stone seats in various parts of the theatre and sense the ghosts, whispers of past entertainments there. The place still has the power to inspire.

'Max has photos of the theatre to show you taken many years ago when I last played there. It was a thrilling experience and will be again, I have no doubt about that.'

Laurent could see in her eyes, hear in her voice, the kindling of excitement, youth and vivacity as she talked about the amphitheatre. It was clear to him that what Eden wanted was to leave her mark on history in that place as so many had before her. And why not? he thought. He was enchanted by her passion for the place and suggested, 'What you're saying is that the Gods of Epidaurus speak to you. How lucky you are.'

Eden was delighted with his understanding. 'What do you know of the Gods of Epidaurus?'

'Nothing, but if they are going to speak to me as they do you, I had better find out about them,' he quipped.

Eden sensed that he was not merely being facetious. She walked across the room to him and filled his glass with champagne. She felt the same way about Laurent she always had. She loved him, still found him sexually appealing, liked being loved by him, wanted to share the best part of herself with him.

Max did not miss that look of affection towards Laurent. It had always been there for him. He understood it because Eden used it on him as well. The problem for Max was the same as for Laurent: they always wanted more from Eden than she was prepared to give. He suggested, 'Let's take our drinks out on the terrace and share them with those Greek gods who speak to you, Eden.'

There was a lovely breeze coming off the sea. The three leaned against the crumbling stone balustrade and watched in silence as the nearly full moon sent its beams down across the sea.

Eden broke the silence between them. 'According to legend, Asklepios was the son of Apollo and Koronis the daughter of the King of Orchomenos. Asklepios was nurtured by a goat after his mother died in childbirth and brought up by the centaur Chiron who taught him the art of healing. He was closely connected with the earth and his symbol was the snake. He, along with Apollo, was worshipped in Epidaurus. In ancient times sick people streamed into the sanctuary there to pray for healing. After various purifications they had to spend a night in the Abaton where the god would appear to them in a dream and indicate the appropriate therapy. He was a good god, Laurent, and though legend is only legend, I do believe he speaks to me, heals me, and playing there is like a payment to the gods for all the good things I have had in my life. If that sounds fanciful, so be it. I only know that some spirit in Epidaurus moves me. Oh, it's true I could have chosen half a dozen other venues in the world, several in Greece, more than one here in Egypt, but Epidaurus is the place I choose for my return. Others, I hope, will follow. I need to give my libation of music to the gods. I somehow think you understand my feelings.'

It was true, Laurent did understand her sentiments. He had always known how grateful Eden was to have such a profound musical talent. One of the things he'd admired about her was that she understood that music is something innate and internal, in her case a creative gift attached to an unerring intuition and enriched by her capacity for profound emotion. He suddenly understood what he had missed when they had first been together. Eden possessed a rich emotional inner world that made her whole and complete. He loved her for it now more than he ever had.

Chapter 10

Eden could not sleep. From the heat? The excitement of preparing for the concerts? Or maybe seeing Laurent again and knowing that he still loved her, was still attracted to her in a sensual way. She was certain of that, had seen it in his eyes and in the manner in which he had caressed her on the beach. It was impossible for her to decide which of these queries was disturbing the rest she was so in need of. Sleepless nights were a torment to Eden. She was one of those people thoroughly unnerved by sleep deprivation. There was, too, another question that kept her tossing and turning in bed. It loomed large and kept her on edge. Her sexual attraction to Laurent . . . She had thought that dead long ago. From the day she ran off with Garfield and all the years after she had never thought of Laurent in these terms. For her he was in the past and that was not a place to dwell in. Now, seeing this ten years older Laurent, had aroused her libido.

Eden knew that he was in the next room, that he would be receptive if she went to him. But she wasn't sure that she wanted to. Such a bold move was not her style. She actually could not imagine how she would handle the situation if she were the one to initiate a sexual move towards him so she tried blocking any thought of sex with Laurent out of her mind and finally fell asleep.

It was a light and disturbed sleep and she came out of it when she heard the door of her room open and saw Laurent move towards her by the moonlight falling across the floor. She sat up against the pillows and drew aside the white mosquito netting draped tent-like from the ceiling over the bed.

'I promised myself at dinner that I would not do this, I would make you crawl to me for sex if you wanted me. And look, here I am,' he told her in a voice brimming with emotion.

'Now look at me,' said Eden as she stood up on the bed and removed her nightgown then got down on her hands and knees and crawled to the edge. She untied the sash around his white silk robe. He opened it and dropped it to the floor then climbed on to the bed as Eden made room for him by crawling backwards.

That was all they had to say to each other. From the moment the mosquito netting was released and fell into place they were cocooned in a chrysalis of sexual ecstasy.

Tonight's sex with Laurent was like nothing she had ever had with him before. He devoured her with kisses deep into her mouth then over every inch of her flesh while he used his hands to excite her, his erect and formidable penis skimming over her body, teasing between the outer lips of her cunt. He toyed with her by slowly, ever so slowly, easing into her then withdrawing, each time a little bit further until she begged him to complete the entry, she so yearned to be filled by his hard and pulsating member.

Laurent was more excited by her than ever he'd expected to be. She kept coming in rapid orgasms, one after the other, where she could hardly catch her breath. When he finally gave in and thrust deep and hard into her she called out so loudly that he had to place a hand over her mouth. He felt her grab him tight with her cunt on his penis and the pleasure was so immense he thought for a moment he would be unable to continue. His natural instinct now that they were in the throes of fucking saved him. Laurent found his rhythm and penetrated and withdrew with a passion for sex he had not had for years. Eden joined him with every thrust so as to make it more exciting for him. They found one different position to fuck by after the other. Eden gave herself up to Laurent, only too delighted to give him every sexual pleasure she could. When he had her on her knees and took her from behind, the penetration was so deep and pleasurable for her that she began to cry. Her tears had nothing to do with his roughness and the moments of heightened sexuality so strong as to be akin to pain his lust was causing her. He had transported her to a sexual nirvana one would give anything and everything to reach. Pure bliss.

He found a way to enter both her most intimate orifices and her pleasure ran over the edge of lust while

Laurent was transported to another world, the world of erotic salvation. He came not once but three times before they were both sated. They lay and caressed each other with the sexual elixir they had between them created. Eden and Laurent never spoke to each other. Neither of them seemed able to verbalise their feelings. Words after such bliss seemed superfluous.

It was dawn when Eden woke. She reached over to touch her lover but he was gone. It suddenly seemed right, very right, that he was not there. Eden sensed that he never would be again and fell asleep, this time into a deep and dreamless state.

Max and Eden were at breakfast when Laurent appeared. He walked straight to Eden, raising first one hand and then the other to kiss them. When they gazed into each other's eyes there was kindness, love, affection, enough so that yet again no words were needed. They sensed they would never discuss what had passed between them the night before.

Eden, Max and Laurent spent the day together working out the programme for the appearances at Epidaurus. They swam in the sea, dined together, walked the beach. But always the three of them. Until they had gone to bed. This time Eden was awake when Laurent entered the room.

The men were gone when Eden went down to breakfast the next morning. It was no surprise, they had discussed their departure with her the night before. She thought of Laurent. Memories of sex with him could not easily be put aside. It had been thrilling. She felt every inch the loved and adored woman, newly sensual. It was marvellous to be erotically desirable once again and to such a young and handsome man.

After breakfast she practised for several hours. Eden had always been her own most savage critic but knew she was playing incredibly well now. She had no doubt that she would give an extraordinarily vital performance at Epidaurus. It was not arrogance that made her feel that way so much as an abiding belief that destiny was at work and she had only to play along with what was meant to be.

From the very first time she had made a trip to Egypt with her mother and father the country had always held an exotic and romantic place in her heart. Every few years she would return. She found it a place that touched her deeply, excited her imagination, was remote from the world she lived in. There was a sweetness and vulnerability about the Egyptian people, an innocence, she found appealing and easy to live with while she was admired by the more sophisticated Egyptians among whom she had many friends. Over the years she had given charity concerts at the Opera House and at the foot of the pyramids in Ghiza. The proceeds built an eye clinic in Cairo, funded a program for visiting nurses in Luxor, created an orphanage and a school in Alexandria.

Eden had always insisted that outside Egypt Max was to play down her good works. They were very private, personal to her, something important she did not want to be exploited in any way. Egypt held a special significance for her as a place both of work and play and that was why it was the place she chose to visit after Hydra on the quest to rejuvenate her life.

For several days after Laurent and Max had left she remained in Magdi's villa practising, walking along the near-deserted beach and re-evaluating all the things that had happened to her in the few weeks since that fateful lunch at Frog's Hollow. It was all happening so fast that the ten-year hiatus she had subjected herself to made her feel as if she had been drugged in some way and merely sleepwalking through those years.

Eden did not miss sex with Sebastian or Sotiri, but she did miss sex with Laurent. It had been exciting beyond measure because emotions such as love and commitment that she knew Laurent wanted from her were for the time being banished. Overpowering erotic desire was what had gripped them and they had indulged in it. The aura still lingered all around her.

Magdi called her every day from Paris. They had not seen each other in several years but had always kept in communication. Now he was returning to Alexandria and made it clear it was only to see her. Eden knew that her routine would be shattered and it would be party time, then, including travel to Upper Egypt. She wondered what Magdi would think of her nowadays. They had, before her affair with Garfield, been lovers but in these past ten years he had not shown any interest in her sexually. She felt quite nervous about his return. Would he want her as he once had, as an exciting, sensuous woman? That was after all what she wanted to be, why she was revisiting the places of her past where she had never been invisible to a man.

The villa was suddenly a hive of activity all around her. The master of the house was expected. Her privacy was at an end. But she had accomplished much and was ready for playtime and a few adventures. It was time to visit the school she'd endowed and all the lost and abandoned children she had rescued.

Magdi arrived just as she was about to drive off on an outing. Already seated in the back of the 1934 Daimler that was placed at her disposal with Gamal as chauffeur, she all but jumped from the seat to greet Magdi as he alighted from the vintage Rolls-Royce that had met him at the airport. Eden was incredibly happy to see her old friend. They kissed and with arms around each other's waist walked up the stairs where all the servants stood waiting to attention. He greeted each and every one of the staff with kind words and a keen interest as to how each of them was and extended his thanks for their taking care of the house and his honoured guest.

Eden watched the expressions of joy on each of the servants' faces. Magdi had the ability to make everyone feel happy. There was a generosity of spirit in the man that was infectious. At last alone in the drawing room with Eden he told her, 'You look marvellous, transformed from how you were the last time we met. You must tell me everything.'

She laughed, amused by his request. Of course he would want to know everything. All Alexandrians, men as well as women, adored gossip. It was a pastime they held in high esteem. 'Yes, but not now. I was on my way into town to visit the children. They're expecting me and I don't want to keep them waiting. Come with me?'

Magdi accepted the invitation without hesitation. He too was one of the patrons of the orphanage and delighted at any time to visit the children, most especially with Eden.

On their arrival they were greeted by the headmistress of the school and the director of the orphanage. Eden never quite knew why these visits were always an emotional experience for her. She always supposed because these were the children she'd never had.

These were the privileged few of the lost children of Egypt. There was, of course, a substantial music department for those talented and interested. On this visit Eden was treated to an 'impromptu' concert that must have been carefully planned for ages and merely waiting for her to appear before being performed.

The children's concert of the Wabi Sharif Institute brought tears to Eden's eyes while Magdi was choked with emotion. Eden had fashioned the music department after Yehudi Menuhin's school for talented violinists in England. The more intellectual society ladies who lunched in Alexandria had worked miracles to raise money for the Institute. They had really taken over what Eden had started and she was indebted to them for their support. Magdi, of course, was a guiding light to them and without his patronage the initiative would have failed. He had political savvy and knew how to cut a swathe through the miles of red tape necessary to get anything done in Egypt.

The bright sunlight, blue skies, and steamy heat are all conducive to a lazy and fun life in Alexandria. The Yacht Club and the various other clubs that Alexandrians frequented made this the ideal playground for Eden, one like nowhere else in the world. She enjoyed the luxury of playing with life while she was here but it could become boring if she was at it too long. She was, after all, a working woman. Work had been her life. Playtime, whether in Egypt or anywhere else, was only a momentary escape from what was essentially an artist's life. The only one that made sense for her. She had sacrificed much – marriage, having her own children – for the excitement and adventure her musical talent brought her.

The coffee house of any city or town in Egypt is always the hub of activity, the place people seek out to get away from the sun, parch their thirst for gossip as well as a cool beverage or delicious sweet. The women were all beautifully turned out in chic Paris couture or New York labels: Calvin Klein, Ralph Lauren, Donna Karan. They were coiffed daily and always made up, as chic a group of pampered women as one will find anywhere. They were also uncommonly nice to one another and particularly to visiting strangers, especially one who was a success of any kind in the working world: an archaeologist, doctor, diplomat, or a great name in music or art circles was always a good excuse for an interesting dinner party. It was almost unheard of for any couple or family to dine without guests.

The Egyptian women who had befriended Eden had one object in life: to be as beautiful and interesting to their husbands and lovers as possible, and always in control of their children whom they wanted to receive the education they themselves had missed. Their personal grooming was made easy for them by the many beauticians, hairdressers and masseuses who came to their houses and bathed them in marvellous scented oils, massaged and pedicured them to perfection, all for pennies compared to beauty upkeep anywhere else in the world. These were females from a different era. Most of them could still remember the glamorous times when Farouk was fresh in memory as King, when princes and pashas had still run the country and its social life. They were around when Laurence Durrell wrote the *Alexandrian Quartet* and captured life there so perfectly. A different world existed now but whenever possible they lived in the old one to which they had been born.

These were the wealthy Egyptians, a minority group compared to the poverty-ridden souls who eked out a living: the country peasant who worked the land, the uneducated who for the most part were being dragged into the twenty-first century kicking and screaming, and those who simply preferred the ancient ways of life on the fringes of or in the desert.

Magdi loved Alexandria. He always seemed to Eden to be happiest when he was here and just slightly out of place when he was abroad. She was delighted to be in his company again. Eden was aware that he was looking

at her as he once had, interested in her from a romantic
and sexual view. She slipped her arm through his and
snuggled closer to him in the rear of the car, kissing him
lightly on the cheek, grateful to him for wanting her in
that way again.

'Where are we going now?' she asked.

'That's up to you. I thought I would take you to
lunch at Pastroudis. Unless you would rather go home?'

It was the look of lust in his eyes that told her home
meant lunch and an afternoon of sex, but grateful as she
was for him wanting her in that way again she was not
ready to resume anything sexual with Magdi. Why she
had not figured out. Too many years of his not wanting
her? Maybe she had had enough sex in the past few
weeks? Or was she sensing that running from one sexual
partner to the other was not the answer to her quest?
There were too many unanswered questions so she told
him, 'It's years since I have been to Patroudis. Let's stop
first at the bar of the Cecil for a gin and tonic.'

Magdi smiled at the suggestion about stopping at the
Hotel Cecil. It was the place where he'd first met Eden.
And so in silence the two of them rode along the
Corniche to the hotel that overlooked the Eastern
harbour. It was a small place of eighty-three rooms that
had had its hey-day before and during the Second World
War. Now it limped along as a nostalgic venue to stay or
more especially to meet in the bar.

One stepped from the car into the sun and heat and
up the few stairs to the entrance to be immediately
swallowed up in the dark coolness of the lobby: a place

of dusty palm trees, a little worn out like the carpets and the open lift, cooled by the blades of the whirling ceiling fans. The welcome here was friendly and served up by the many white-robed and turbaned *sufragis* and the concierge who had been there for as long as Eden could remember.

The sight of Magdi and his guest brought the concierge and the hotel manager from behind their stations. For Eden the Cecil was a home away from home, or at least had been in her past. She had even brought Garfield here while giving one of her recitals in Alexandria.

The bar was nearly empty, the barman effusive in his pleasure to see them again. As they sat and drank Magdi and Eden relived old memories.

'Remember the night we met?' he asked.

'Every detail. I had been to a party at the Yacht Club for a Saudi prince. He found me irresistible and sent a flunkey around to invite me to his rooms. He assumed I would be thrilled by the invitation. When I declined it, and I might add most graciously, his go-between told me, "It would be very foolish for you to reject an invitation from the Prince. If he wants you, he will have you."

'When I told him, "Don't be ridiculous," he kissed my hand and told me, "You will see." I forgot all about it and enjoyed my evening with friends though they did not laugh off the invitation as I did.

'When we arrived here at the Cecil, the door was locked. My escort rang the bell and it was opened. He insisted on seeing me safely to the lift. It was so quiet in the lobby. I remember thinking the staff on duty seemed twitchy then told myself it was just my imagination. Stepping out of the lift, I passed you in the hall. You waited for the boy to let me into my room and return to take you down in the lift. I remember thinking he was unusually nervous. Once he'd put the lights on and lowered the shutter to the balcony he all but fled from the room. I only had time to kick off my shoes when the door to the hall burst open and the boy dashed back in and shot the bolt on the door connecting the room next door to mine. Then he pulled me by the hand towards the hall and kept repeating, "Sorry, sorry." I kept pulling back, trying to stay in my room. Then you came to my rescue. The prince had had someone pay the boy to open the door between the two rooms. He was going to be in the adjoining one. I remember so well your paying off the boy and telling me it was not safe for me to stay at the Cecil until the prince was out of Alexandria. So I went home with you. It all seems so funny now but that night it was sinister.'

'It took him years to forgive me. And still a decade after the incident he was saying I probably did you a disservice. You might have been a princess now.'

From the Cecil they went to Pastroudis where they dined on the seafood for which Alexandria is noted: endless platters of large grilled shrimp served with lemon and butter, a mound of aromatic buttered rice and a bottle of Montrachet. There they saw many of Magdi's friends and in minutes caught up on all the scandal, who at the moment was having an affair with whom.

Eden and Magdi, of course, were being gossiped about themselves.

And with good reason. For as much as Eden had decided to not go to bed with Magdi, her resistance was low and that first night when they returned to his villa, they made love to one another. It was sex with more affection and satisfaction than she'd thought she would achieve ever again in his arms. There were no bad memories to be caught up in as there had been with Laurent yet more than the mere sexual gratification that had come from the night with Sotiri and Sebastian. Magdi's and Eden's was a sexual reunion that worked for both of them. He was very sexy and adventurous in bed, met his match in Eden and loved her for it. He had after all been the one to introduce her to the wild side of sex where things she'd never dreamed of could bring on heightened orgasm, where she lost every inhibition, where there were no taboos.

However, after several days the same old feeling of wasting time interfered with Eden's playtime and she was back to practising and thinking about her concerts at Epidaurus and of feeling no longer invisible but whole, looking and feeling the woman she had once been and still was.

Chapter 11

'It's time I was thinking of going home, back to my house in England. The wild flowers will be up from their winter sleep, the orchard will soon be a blaze of pink, and I have a great deal to do before my concerts. But I always find it a wrench to leave Egypt,' Eden told her host.

'We haven't been on a trip yet. You can't leave before we make a few excursions. Where would you like to go?' asked Magdi.

They decided to motor to the Wadi el Natrun, sixty-three miles south-west of Alexandria, their objective to visit the monks who lived in a complex of monasteries near the Natrun oasis that dated from the second century AD. It was a very special desert place that received few visitors, the monks disliking intrusion of any sort from outside.

Magdi and Eden had been there before and it was for her one of the special places in the world. The atmosphere of the visits never left her. She carried the stillness of the desert, the passion of the monks to live only for

God, with her every day of her life. She had been inspired previously by the monks and the monasteries, believing that this was the place on earth closest to God. It had so marked her that one of her compositions for the cello and two violins inspired by Wadi el Natrun had had critics acclaiming it as 'God's music'. It was one of her finest works.

And so the boot of Magdi's car was loaded with fruit and sweets, a sack of flour, sugar and salt, a case of wine, a carton of candles as gifts for the monks, and a hamper of luscious food for a picnic for Eden, Magdi and any of the monks prepared to accept Magdi's hospitality. That was always hard to predict as for the most part they followed the ascetic rule, not living for food or luxury of any kind.

Eden decided that she would take her cello with her and, if they so desired, would play the piece that they and the Wadi el Natrun had inspired her to write.

They set off at five o'clock in the morning when it was cool and so they might have a full day of stepping into another world and time, for the four Wadi el Natrun monasteries and their ancient ruins were surely that. The Coptic community, Christian Egyptian, had impressed Eden by their devout and austere life in the solitude and serenity of the desert wilderness.

They arrived at ten in the morning with a document signed by the Coptic Patriarchate in Cairo giving them permission to visit. That was the only way an outsider was allowed here. Once more Eden was overwhelmed by the Wadi el Natrun monasteries, the monks, the ruins and the desert. There was a silence here as in no other place on earth. It ate into her soul. The heat and dust choked her and, just as she had on her first visit, she wanted to weep for the power of nothingness, the simplicity of this life, for the ultimate sacrifices that could be made for the love of God.

Here was a place that levelled life out, brought it to the lowest common denominator. What did it really matter after all whether she had felt herself just one of the millions of invisible women? What was this pathetic need to be loved and have a sexual life when confronted with the stillness and peace of the desert and these robed men who lived in a special ecstasy all the time *just* by surrendering the world and all desire?

Eden, Magdi and their driver were greeted warmly once they had produced the document. Until then the monks, the few who could be found or seen, had scuttled away from them. They were offered water from the well. It was cool but tasted of sand, maybe even a little brackish, but it would have been crass not to accept their humble offer of hospitality.

Inside the first monastery they were shown icons, the monks' few treasures of ancient Coptic fragments of robes, bibles and manuscripts. Afterwards they spent several hours talking to the monks about the monastic life in the Wadi el Natrun. They would not indulge themselves in sharing Magdi's picnic but did gratefully accept an invitation to hear Eden play the piece she had written inspired by their life.

Later she left her cello in the monastery and even

with the heat of the day bearing down on them Magdi, Eden and Gamal, accompanied by an elderly monk, trekked under large black silk umbrellas through the desert to a small oasis of several palm trees. There, under the shadow of a tree, they drank chilled beer which seemed the only thing that could quench their thirst and ate roasted pigeon stuffed with buttered cinnamon rice and a Tabouleh salad of wheat, mint and flat-leafed parsley.

After lunch Magdi stretched out on the sand and slept. Eden, however, left the party to walk to the top of a sand dune, quite close by. The monk wanted to follow her for safety reasons. It was too easy to lose one's bearing in the desert. Eden's insistence that she wanted to go alone and her promise not to walk out of sight of the oasis granted her her wish.

Walking in the desert is hard work at the best of times and climbing the dune was very hard work. But climb it she did and her reward was an unobstructed view of dunes undulating away for as far as the eye could see. The silence was profound, like nowhere else in the world. The bareness of a place with not a trace of man or beast to leave so much as a footprint has its own overwhelming beauty. Eden sat down on the summit of the dune with her back to the oasis. For a while, she had no idea for how long, time seemed to have stood still, was no longer relevant. She simply sat looking out at the sea of sand and sky.

The heat beat down from a white sun hanging in a cloudless sky, but it was a dry-as-a-bone sort of heat and there was a hot lazy breeze coming in from somewhere beyond. The heat seemed to beat all thought from her brain, leaving an emptiness that was in itself sublime. Then quite suddenly her mother and father appeared to her almost as a vision. They were the young and beautiful people they had always been; she sensed they still loved her and were happy together wherever they were. The men in her life flashed before her then. She was aware of having loved each of them in a special but transient way. They were forgiving of the loss of her love for them. Only one of them issued a poisonous feeling. It was Garfield and she could not understand why. He, of all the men who had been a part of her life, was the one to whom she had given herself up completely. It was he whom she'd allowed to ruin her life; *he* who'd left *her*.

She felt rather like the drowning man whose life flashes past him before he goes under for the last time. Suddenly they were all gone and Eden felt cleansed by the experience. She could see for the first time that men could not accept her independence. They were used to being the partner who played games of love with their women. They were the ones able to walk away from a relationship when it no longer interested them, and a new one did, without a qualm. All her life *she* had dropped men as men usually drop women and *she* had marched on.

All that . . . here in the desert seemed unimportant and had little to do with the big picture of solitude and sacrifice. She realised that she had always had an appreciation of the life that was right for her and those involved with her. She felt humbled by the desert and grateful that she had never abused the talent that fate had dealt her, that she had sacrificed relationships which had not proved sustaining. Now for the first time she could understand and forgive Garfield for walking out on her, when she could not give him what he wanted. She could even face the fact that she had allowed his dumping her so ruthlessly to take her ten years to get over.

She could faintly hear Magdi calling her from a distance and in a flash all her new awareness slipped into place, settled in her soul and out of her mind.

The heat was relentless. The trek back to the monasteries seemed to Eden to be swifter, easier, than they had experienced on the way to the oasis. There the monks had set up a makeshift canopy of black cloth on four rickety poles for shade for Eden and her cello on a stretch of sand that faced the emptiness of the desert.

After lying down in one of the cells for half an hour she gave her concert to the few resident monks who lived there. She played the piece she had composed inspired by her last visit here, 'Desert Voices', and thought how privileged she was to be able to return to the Wadi el Natrun to play it. The silence, the scent of the desert, the music: Eden knew she would never again have such a profound experience no matter how well she played it or where. Magdi and she were silent all the way back to the villa except when he told her, 'I have never been so moved by a piece of music as I have been today. You are blessed.'

Eden knew that, had always known it. It was what made her humble about what and who she was, why she never abused her talent, why it had always come first in her life above all else. Of all the men who had loved her not one of them understood that the burden of creativity, success, to have the gift of greatness, was what controlled her. Or if they did they hadn't known how to accept it and love her for it. If one of them had, she knew she might have a husband and children now and still be with that man.

The pieces of her past seemed during this journey to be falling into place, making a picture, solving a puzzle. She had a better picture, a more realistic one surely, of her life and herself. Those love affairs had failed because they had run their course, and suddenly that seemed only fitting and right. This was no cheap rationalisation but an understanding so profound and positive that she knew she could now go home. Her career was back on track, so was she as a woman admired by and desirable to men. Love was just around the corner, all she had to do was be on the right street. She smiled and laughed because her life was rich and full and there was the right man out there somewhere for her. She was as sure of it as that the sun would set this evening and rise again in the morning.

That night she and Magdi made love. The sex was as thrilling as ever, the joy of orgasm took Eden over and she experienced sensational pleasure all through the night. In the morning over breakfast she announced to him that she wanted to go home that day.

He arranged her journey and accompanied her to Cairo. There were several hours to wait before her flight and so they decided to go to the Mouski, the old bazaar situated near the street also called the Mouski, the oldest commercial centre in Cairo. Eden and Magdi walked the narrow, picturesque lanes lined with tiny shops, sheltered from the sun by wooden awnings. It teemed with milling crowds and mingled scents. In the streets craftsmen worked in the same manner as their predecessors had five centuries earlier on copperware and ivory. Gold and silver jewellery was displayed in dirty windows. Perfume, gems, spices and silk were arranged in the shops and out in the lanes. Offers of coffee enticed people into shops to browse.

The Mouski is made up of several *souqs*, markets or bazaars, the best of which is the Khan al Khalili. That was where Magdi and Eden were headed, not to shop but to visit a cafe, Feshawi's, perhaps the most famous tea and coffee shop in Cairo. Its atmosphere transports a visitor centuries back into the past. Feshawi's has a tradition of being especially popular during the month of Ramadan, particularly around midnight when it is full and lively. Eden had spent many a late evening there with the intellectual and political friends she had made in Cairo. It was where they gathered to gossip and exchange ideas. The smoke from the water pipes and cigarettes mingled with the scent of the Khan Khalili: garlic, spices, all sorts of heavy floral perfumes. It was reflected in the many gold-framed full-length pier glasses hung on the walls reflecting people so that the small area seemed always to be packed with patrons. It was here that the Egyptian musicians would have met, where the Alexandrian poet C.P. Cavafy would have spent his time when visiting Cairo, where on visiting Egypt Tennessee Williams and his entourage would take up several of the small round marble-topped tables. It was the Deux Magots of the Middle East.

They were greeted with enthusiasm by the white-robed and turbaned staff who recognised them and showed them to a table named after Matisse, next to one they referred to as Picasso. Eden and Magdi might have had one called Mafouz but Feshawi's only whispered that was where he sat because Egypt's famous novelist was still alive and usually there with a friend.

Feshawi's was a meeting place but also a crossroads where one might expect to meet anyone from the past or present. But the last people Eden had ever expected to meet were Garfield and Dante. She had always known that one day their paths would cross and had wondered how she would feel then, what she would do. There had been many imagined scenarios but not the one that was happening now.

The two men were sitting further back in the long narrow cafe, accompanied by a well-known American writer whom Eden had met when she was with Garfield. They had taken an instant dislike to one another. Eden felt weak-kneed. She wanted to turn away and flee from Feshawi's but she seemed unable to move. Magdi led her by the elbow to the table offered to them and they sat down. He had not seen Garfield and only did once he had been seated. He and Eden were in an awkward position. To flee from the cafe would be a sign of weakness. There was nothing to do but sit it out.

After the initial shock of seeing Garfield in Feshawi's of all the places in the world she might have bumped into him, Eden composed herself with a massive effort. It took several minutes for the colour to return to her face.

'Do you want to leave?' asked Magdi.

'Certainly not. It was bound to happen that I should bump into him somewhere. No, certainly not, let *him* leave.'

Eden listened to herself and her words gave her strength and the ability to put this unfortunate meeting into perspective. She turned her attention to Magdi and the coffee and sweets that had been placed in front of her.

'Are you all right? You seem to be,' he said.

Eden heard the concern for her in his voice. She appreciated his loyalty and wanted to dispel his anxiety. 'Yes, I'm quite all right. I can assure you Garfield will never upset me again. Nor will I allow him to spoil anything for me, not for five minutes. The most dreadful thing about seeing him is that there is still chemistry between us. I still find him incredibly attractive from a sexual point of view. There is something about him I want to love, even now, but I will never let that happen again. He was the great love of my life but that's over.

'Magdi, I'm indebted to you for many things but taking me to the Wadi el Natrun yesterday has to stand

154

out as one of the great experiences of my life. Possibly the greatest. Something very deep and abiding and at the same time mystical happened to me while I was sitting on that sand dune, giving myself up to the emptiness of the desert. My life, past and present, came together before my very eyes. So I loved and lost Garfield? It never really mattered in the big picture of life. It was never meant to be, it just took me a long time to understand that.'

Magdi looked across the room into one of the tall slender gilt-framed mirrors. There he had an excellent view of Garfield and Dante, the back of the other man. He could well understand Eden's attraction to her former lover. He was handsome, smooth, intelligent and very sexy. He was also evil.

Magdi turned his attention back to Eden. 'Garfield has made a profession out of sex and love. He is a taker, but you always knew that. Just try and remember all the good times you gave each other and forget you ever loved him.'

'Good advice,' she told him and leaned over to kiss him on the cheek.

Fortunately an old friend of Magdi's entered Feshawi's then and on seeing him and Eden joined them. A very amusing man, he had Eden and Magdi laughing with his gossiping and story telling. Eden soon forgot that Garfield was across the room from them. Then quite suddenly he was standing next to her, seeking her hand so he could lower his head to press a kiss upon it.

Garfield the consummate gigolo had not been taken

aback on seeing Eden. His immediate reaction was that she looked marvellous, ten years hardly showed on her. He was surprised that the chemistry between them was still there. He wanted her, in bed, in his life, suddenly missed all that they'd had together. Charm oozed from every pore in his body. He went into gigolo overdrive.

'How marvellous you look,' he told her, still holding the hand he had kissed.

'I often wondered how it would be and where, when next we were to meet,' she told him, fighting back the dizzying joy of being next to him again. 'You remember Magdi?'

The two men shook hands and Magdi introduced Garfield to his friend.

'Where are you staying?' he asked Eden.

'I'm not. I'm flying to Rome and then on to London this afternoon,' she told him. Then wrenched her hand from his and stood up.

Magdi immediately took the hint and rose from his chair. He called for the bill and excused himself to his friend for leaving so abruptly.

They were in the street but still in front of Feshawi's when Garfield accosted Eden again. Magdi was talking to a shopkeeper he knew who was passing by as the two of them had come out of the cafe.

'I want to see you! Don't tell me that the chemistry between us has vanished because I don't believe it. I would like to whisk you away right now and remind you of how great we were together. Don't tell me you wouldn't like that, that you don't feel the same way?'

Eden was overwhelmed by the charisma of the man: his physical beauty, the scent of his body, the shock of dirty blond hair streaked with white from the sun, the chiselled face. She looked into his eyes. They instantly dispelled her attraction to him. She could see the evil in them, the selfishness, the hunger. She imagined his thoughts about her whirring through his brain: how he would get her into bed and fuck her into oblivion, move in on her because she was grateful for the erotic life they had together, because she still loved him and was helpless to walk away, how he could manipulate her to grant him his every wish no matter how demeaning it might be for her. She had after all done so once before. She sensed the power of his ability to manipulate under the smooth pretence of being humble. How had she not seen all that before? That he was a pretender *par excellence*.

She removed his arm from hers, looked up into his face and told him, 'Of course I would like that. I do feel the same way. Garfield, there's no need for you to whisk me away to remind me of what we had together. It was the best. But I paid too dearly for it. Too much ever to let us happen again: not for love, not for a fuck. What after all was my attraction to you? A chance to play with the devil? To be loved and fuck my brains out with a decadent, disloyal bastard? To become a masochist because I was too spoiled and innocent to understand that you loved me sadistically, if not towards my body then my mind? To have you resent me for my successes and because I loved you for what you were? And last but not least to have you once again run away from me because there was nothing more for you to get out of me?

'Oh, yes, I always knew what you were but I allowed my passion for you to blind me. I was accustomed to good people, real people with genuine feelings who knew how to love. How was I to recognise or understand those who are not? I loved you once. Now go find another victim.'

Eden tried to walk away but Garfield grabbed her by the arm. She was carrying a lizard handbag which she swung and hit him across the face. He was so stunned he released her and she quite calmly walked away.

Chapter 12

Eden adored Italy, especially Tuscany. There had been such happy times there with her mother and father, a Florentine count having proved to have been one of Leila's longest and best affairs. It was Alberto Chimini who had given Eden her cello, a Stradivarius dating from the 1670s. The cello had been cut down in length but not in width a hundred years before. It was more like a Montagano cello, quite big and heavy. Eden used, on occasion, to refer to it as her brute. The brute had always been the correct cello for her because she was such a forceful player. It had, however, been suggested that it did not have the response of a freshly preserved instrument. The brute was over bass-orientated with a limited carrying power on the top strings.

Count Chimini had remained one of her most loyal and supportive patrons. He was inordinately proud of what she had achieved and had offered many times to buy her a new cello. To that end he had bought a remarkable Strad called the Surabaya. It had been crafted during Stradivarius's golden period and was slightly smaller than the brute. The instrument had a fantastic pedigree that was well documented; it also carried with it a romantic story. The Count had bought it for Eden just at the time she decided to give up performing in public. It was such a magnificent gift she felt she could not accept it unless there was an audience who could appreciate the beauty of its sound.

The Count was waiting for her with his car at Rome airport. She was met at the luggage carousel by his friend, Carlo Marcelli, a man of considerable years who had known Eden since she was a young girl. They greeted each other with a hug, a kiss of the hand on his part. '*Cara mia,* he is waiting in the car for you and so happy you're here.'

The Count lived in great luxury and incredible chic. They drove for half an hour to his villa on the outskirts of Rome, a beautiful family house with magnificent gardens. The staff were dressed in his family's livery which included white gloves and seemed to be standing around in pairs everywhere.

Eden and the Count were both so excited about her at last accepting the cello that everything else was forgotten. They went to the music room where the cello was kept under a glass case along with the other rare instruments the Count collected. Eden had played the Surabaya many years ago so she knew what a marvellous instrument it was. There were technical disadvantages to an instrument with gut strings but Eden always favoured them because they commanded a greater warmth and individual beauty. She was aware that gut does not respond quickly to the bow, that it is supple and beyond a certain degree will not resist pressure. She knew that with this instrument she would have to limit her power even more than when playing the brute which also had gut strings.

The moment she took the Surabaya in her hands she fell in love with it. She sat down and played it. All she could say to Alberto Chimini after hearing the sound was, 'Alberto, are you certain you want to give me the Surabaya? It is one of the really great instruments of the world.'

'I always meant it to be played by the finest cellist. It was bought for you, remember. Your mother was alive then and she said, "Alberto, I will always love you for doing this for Eden. It means that you recognise her along with the greatest musicians or I know you would never give her such an important instrument." So the Surabaya was bought and put away for the day you would come and claim it. Too bad my dear Leila is not with us to hear you play this glorious Strad.'

Once again the Count turned out to be a most generous benefactor. Eden stayed with him for several days and they had an orgy of magnificent music. The more she played the Surabaya, the more in love with it she fell. It offered an exquisite palate of musical colours. The Count's love and knowledge of music prompted Eden to discuss her planned concert at Epidaurus. They went over the programme and he offered several excellent suggestions.

Eden knew that her mother had been the real true

love of his life; that he was doing this in her memory as much as because he believed Eden to be one of greatest cellists the world had ever known. He had never asked her why she had stopped playing in public and he never asked her now why she was making a comeback, he was too much of a gentleman for that. What he did sense was that she would never retire from the stage again unless she was forced to. He would be there in Epidaurus.

They kissed goodbye at the airport and there were tears of joy in their eyes at the emotion that surged through them, the love of great music.

Eden and her two cellos were settled comfortably in first-class seats to London. She was drinking a glass of champagne and settling down at last from her state of excitement over her visit to Alberto and having accepted the Surabaya.

It was only after the second glass that she thought of how well she had always been received in Italy. The men there had found her beautiful and sexy and had no qualms about showing it. Even on this trip when she had been in town with the Count for brief visits she was aware of the admiring glances she received from men and women alike. Alberto, noticing too, had remarked, 'You can still draw the men and I have no doubt you will do the same for your audience.'

Eden smiled, remembering her younger days, her concerts in Rome and Milan, Naples and Florence, and the many Italian lovers she'd had: brief encounters, exciting romantic sex. Those had been the days of miniskirts and promiscuity. Her long and shapely legs in sheer black or white stockings acted like a magnet to the dark and sexy Italian musicians, including two famous tenors who competed for a night with her.

At the outset of this odyssey Eden had wanted to go to the places where she had been a success as a woman as well as a cellist. She had had no intention of trying to recapture the loves of her life so she had not looked up any of the men who had played that role. Memory can do wonders for one's ego and more than that it can remind one of what was real and what one imagined to be real. She was delighted to have been right about returning to places of those days where she had flirted and toyed with men and sex. This journey had reached into her soul and brought back what had been there all the time, the same sensuous person who adored sex in its many and varied ways, the brilliant cellist and composer loved and adored by her public and who the critics constantly admired and were confused by.

It had always been a burden for Eden to bear, making her a fish out of water so to speak, that she was a slim beauty who all her life looked more like a well-groomed Hollywood star or a rebellious deb rather than a stuffy, serious musician. She could thank her mother for that and other lessons learned from Leila: that she must always satisfy her female yearnings, play the woman's role as well as the artist's, be a complete human being, a whole soul. When still a teenager Eden knew she had the reputation of being a sexy beauty and her personal life was gossiped about: the many men, the affairs, her flirtatious way of getting everything she wanted, the fool she made of herself later by loving Garfield so.

What she had not realised was that that was who she was, and if her genius caused people to talk about her, well, so what? It had never bothered her when she was young, only when she had been with Garfield and after he'd left her, as she became an older woman. Sitting on the plane, her two cellos by her side, Eden Sidd raised her glass and silently made a toast: Goodbye to the old age syndrome which nearly killed me off for good.

In London she was met by Max. He was astonished and delighted to see her walk through the doors of the customs hall with a porter pushing a luggage wagon carrying two cello cases. Immediately he knew she had at last accepted the Surabaya. Another titbit to feed the press about the Eden Sidd comeback.

When she had spoken to Max from the Count's villa, she had raved that the Surabaya was a glorious instrument to play but had said nothing about accepting it as a gift. She did, however, the moment he took her in hand at the airport tell him, 'Wait until you hear the golden rounded sound the Surabaya gives off.'

He added, 'And we must remember there is that unique Eden Sidd sound too. I can hardly wait to hear you play Schubert's Trout on the Surabaya. The bow – what bow did he give you?'

'Two, my dear Max, can you credit it? A Dodd and a Palormo. They are both absolutely marvellous. His generosity always overwhelms me.'

Max and Eden had dinner at the Ivy. A luscious very expensive dinner: lobster soufflé to begin with then veal in a cream and mushroom sauce, miniature vegetables, and a dark rich chocolate dessert with double cream oozing from it. They drank champagne all through the meal. It was after all a celebration in honour of the new Stradivarius. After dinner, Max had his chauffeur drive them to Eden's house.

Immediately on seeing the village she had the sensation of having been away years rather than months. So much had happened to her in such a short time. There was the old fire raging in her once more to live life to the fullest. The house was aglow with lamplight, it looked inviting and she was pleased to be home. As they approached the entrance to her house she had the distinct impression that she was not returning as the same person who had left. Those last ten years in the house seemed like a dream she had sleepwalked through. It was disconcerting.

'It's nearly one o'clock in the morning. Rachel will have gone home and taken the dogs with her. She knew I was returning but not at what time.'

Max took her keys and opened the door. On entering the house a sense of uneasiness came over Eden. She actually felt light-headed. She was happy to be there but everything seemed strange, as if she were seeing her things and the rooms for the first time. She tried to remember other times in the kitchen, the drawing room, the music room, but as soon as she pictured them they drifted away from her. Memories of her years in the house simply did not exist, or if they did the Eden of today could not identify with them.

Once she and the cellos were settled in, she made tea. That was even more odd because she knew where everything was yet it seemed as if she were making tea in that kitchen for the first time.

Max asked, 'Are you all right? You seem to be somewhere else.'

'I'm fine, fine. Just overtired, ready for bed,' she told him, a small white lie. Eden could not explain to Max that she no longer felt like the same woman who had lived here for ten years. It was too bizarre. He would never understand.

She had always been proud of herself for not being highly strung, of being well grounded and able to take things in their stride. This sensation she was having now quite threw her. It was not like her at all. Normally she would have asked Max if he wanted to stay the night but she truly needed to be alone so apologised for not asking him and sent him on his way.

All the way back to London Max thought about Eden. How much he still loved her. He marvelled that it was as strong a love as it had ever been. He had found it difficult when in Alexandria to accept that she was entering a new phase in her life and he would remain as he had always been her constant friend and nothing more. There was a change in her. Instinct told him she was at last ready to settle her private life with marriage if the right man came along. It hurt him to concede that he was not even in the running. And what of Laurent? And Magdi? Garfield? She had loved them all at some time or another and surely Laurent was still there for the picking. Magdi, Max knew, would never work, he was too much of a libertine, would never stay faithful. She still loved Garfield but was she self-destructive enough to settle for him? Max doubted that. Then for one brief moment hope for himself soared like a bird on wing. But that had happened so many times in the twenty years he had known her he swiftly put it out of his mind. The fact of the matter was that if he and Eden had not had sex together by now, it was never going to happen.

His brief moment vanished and he concentrated on the concert at Epidaurus, even took notes of things that had to be done immediately. He had secured the amphitheatre, booked Laurent, the Boston Symphony miraculously were free for when he wanted them, they were negotiating fees and contracts were being drawn up. He had worked miracles because orchestras, concert halls and conductors were usually booked solid for two years in advance. The enthusiasm and co-operation he was receiving for Eden's comeback was astonishing. But then he had always known how disappointed the music world had been when she suddenly retired.

Laurent, on returning from Alexandria, went directly into a heavy work program. Concerts, marvellous music and great artists filled his life but every day his thoughts turned to Eden. If it wasn't her artistry on the cello then it was his nights in her bed he brought back to mind. He tried to put her out of his mind but that was impossible. The sex had been incredibly thrilling and he wanted more of her in that way, but in other ways as well. He wanted her to love him at least as much as he loved her. He was determined not to let her slip away from him once more.

From Max, he learned where she was, what she was doing. Every day he wanted to call her but instinct told him to hold back. Instead he had sent her flowers in Alexandria, and while conducting in New York he bought her an unusual Tiffany watch and sent it to her in Rome. Finally the day after she returned to her house in England he could bear it no longer and called her there.

'There's no use pretending otherwise, I found you as marvellous as ever in Alexandria. I have to know how it was for you?'

'Equally as marvellous, Laurent.'

She paused and he gave a sigh, not so much of relief as of contentment. He closed his eyes and embraced the memory of those nights.

'Laurent?'

'I'm still here. You sound so sexy. It excites me to hear how you feel about sex with me. I always did get a sexual buzz when I heard a certain tone in your voice. I've caught that tone as you tossed it to me just now. The sexual flirt voice, I used to call it. The orgasm voice, the come voice. I wish I could reach out and touch you right now, lick your breasts, suck on your nipples, drink from your cunt, caress your bottom, make you come, give you all the erotic pleasure I can possibly muster. But you know that, don't you?'

'Yes, I know that, my dear. Do you think that I am

any less excited than you are right now? I am not. I am lying on my bed, legs spread and ready to receive the joy sex with you always gives me. Speak to me, tell me all the things you would like to be doing with me. They're very exciting, these erotic telephone conversations we have together, or I should say used to have together. They narrow the distance between us. Do you always come with me during phone sex? I want you to come with me now. I wish I could taste you on my tongue, feel you hard and thick taking possession of me, filling me with the lust you have for me and me alone. Oh, God, I've just come and it's sublime.'

Laurent wanted to weep with joy, shout out to the world how exquisite they were together in sex. So well matched, so willing to serve each other in the erotic world they dwelt in. Eden had always understood how much he needed her to excite him when they were thousands of miles apart. At first she had been hesitant to tease him on the telephone with her sexy voice and lewd talk. But when they had been in love and wanting to be intimate all the time, telephone sex became important in their relationship.

After a while spent turning Laurent on, imagining him coming or merely fondling himself, Eden found the power to control him a turn on for herself. In time she came to look forward to telephone sex with him, coming on her own, enjoyed fondling herself, sighing with the deep satisfaction of selfish one-sided sex, the privacy of it. Laurent adored her even more for being able to come just from their talk.

He used to get such a high from it that he formed a habit of calling Eden from the stage telephone minutes before he would walk out to the already seated orchestra. Many was the time when the audience had to wait while he got his erection under control.

Laurent told her now, 'You can always do it for me like no other woman can.'

'Have there been many other women, Laurent?'

'Many. I would be lying if I said otherwise.'

'I am glad,' she told him.

'What else could I do? You taught me to love sex, made me into an accomplished lover. I may have been heartbroken, my dear, but I wasn't stupid.'

'No, never stupid. I did love you, you know, and then it was over, love had run its course. How many people have you walked away from because a love affair was over? Many more than I have, I am sure of that.'

'That's probably true. So love has run its course for us, is that what you're telling me?'

'No, I said it *had* run its course.'

'And now?

'There is sex and music between us. That is quite enough to begin with, don't you think?' asked Eden flirtatiously.

'I want you to come again – I know you will. Just imagine I am there on top of you, slowly, methodically, fucking you.'

Laurent continued to excite Eden with his own brand of lewd conversation. He offered her sex as rough and ready as if he were a stevedore or a lorry driver, a bricklayer lover, and knew when she had come because she let go that special kind of sigh that only accompanies orgasm.

Chapter 13

It was nearly four weeks since Garfield had had his confrontation with Eden in Cairo. As long as he was busy touring Upper Egypt he'd been able to put it out of his mind. But now that he was back in Paris where every newspaper had something to say about Eden Sidd's comeback, where she was a topic of conversation in the circles he frequented, and most especially the day he saw posters for Epidaurus, that meeting returned to haunt him. Not the confrontation, merely the shock of seeing her again.

It came as something of a surprise to Garfield that he should still want her as much as he did. He had always adored her for being such a great artist, world-class successful. That had been part of his falling in love with her. In Cairo the sexual attraction had been as intense as when they'd first met. Of all the women he had had in his life she was the one for whom he had felt real love. She was the gigolo's bonus, love and great sex as well as another victim to exploit.

Yes, he had exploited her at every turn. It had been a

glorious love affair because she had given him everything. She'd made it so easy by her generosity. She legitimised the dark greedy side of his nature. That was why he pushed further and further, took everything from her. He was able to justify his actions by putting it down to the quirks in his nature, and always maintained he could see nothing wrong in them.

Dante had been right to make him leave her. Love, her kind of love, was a dead loss for a man like him. Yet now, having seen her again, pulling off a great coup for her return, setting herself up for the world to see and hear, and thinking not least about the wealth she would gain from performing again, made Garfield think that he may have made a grave error by dumping her when she was down and struggling. Had he underestimated her? Obviously he had. There was a great deal more to get from loving Eden. No matter what she'd said in the *Souq* in front of Feshawi's, he was confident that she still loved him. He had even said as much.

Garfield pressed his hand to his cheek and remembered the painful bruise Eden had given him when she had hit him with her handbag. Oh, yes, she still loved him, still wanted him. A plan of how to win her back began forming in his mind. She was back in the celebrity market and he was determined to be right there with her.

Memories kept flooding back: how the world had once rushed to embrace them as a beautiful and talented couple, how welcome they had been at gallery openings, musical events, concerts, opera openings. They had made the list for the most interesting dinner and cocktail parties in San Francisco, New York, London, Paris, Berlin.

People had flocked to be invited to their houses in Hydra, her Park Avenue flat in New York, but they had hardly entertained. For the most part Garfield had been happy to keep their life together at home just for them and no one else. How many times had he used the excuse that he didn't want to share her but to keep her to himself? He had enjoyed his life with Eden but at the same time he had been a free agent, had gone out discreetly with other women under the guise of business. The wealthy men and women he cultivated, patrons of the arts, had offered him many and varied rewards. Eden had believed whatever he told her and dutifully stayed at home waiting for him, cooking intimate dinners, making herself attractive and sexy, open and ready for sex at any time he wanted it.

He had always told her that when she was back on her feet he would return to claim her and they would begin again. Well, now was the time for him to make his move. He rang Dante and they made a date to meet in Garfield's studio.

He was already there and painting when he heard his friend's key in the lock. The two men embraced as they always did on meeting. 'Oh, you're getting on again with the dune painting. It's looking marvellous. Have you showed it to Cecile?'

'No, and don't mention it to her. I'm keeping canvasses aside for a show in New York. You know Cecile, she'll want control of them and I don't want her to represent me in New York. We agreed I need better representation there. I'm going to go for the Castelli Gallery. They were interested, or at least Leo said he was. I'm sorry he died but the gallery still goes on and I'm in very well with the women running it. Anyway, work isn't why I asked you to come by. I've decided to go after Eden.'

'I thought that was dead, finished forever?'

'I thought so too. But when I saw her in Cairo, I knew that it wasn't. She's on top again or will be once she plays those comeback performances she's planning.'

'I understand all the seats are sold for both nights at Epidaurus. Such a clever campaign Max has pulled together. Have you seen the posters? They're sensational. So sexy that stance of hers, so outrageous that dress. Valentino, I'm sure. She won't take you back and I don't think you should waste any time trying. I don't believe you love her. You're not going to give me that twaddle about her being the only woman you really loved, are you? Pull yourself together, stick to our plan. We have shows to paint and ladies and gentlemen who want to sponsor you and our lifestyle. You have a wife and son and me, and are attractive to any number of men and women who want to have sex with you. Be smart, my dear, and forget Eden Sidd. If you can't get her out of your head then go for the sex and be done with her is my best advice.'

'Why are you getting so angry over this, Dante?'

'Because Eden Sidd is dangerous. She nearly ruined

our way of life once, she could do it again. She doesn't accept, as your wife and son do, that I am a part of your life and always will be. You nearly abandoned me once because of Eden, I'll not have that happen again. If you love anyone, you love me and your son. And that's the truth of the matter. If you feel a need to have sex with her than just do and leave her. Better still, don't do it and find someone else who can further us.'

Garfield could see how upset Dante was, and that it was not one of his performances. He was full of genuine *angoisse* over the very notion of Garfield trying to win Eden back. He went to Dante and placed an arm round his shoulders, hugging his old friend to him. Garfield stroked his cheek and told him, 'Calm down, we'll do Eden together or I'll drop any further interest in her. I left her for you and our life plan once, I can do it again if I have to. Just listen to my plan because it includes you.'

'Go on then. I can see we'll never be rid of Eden Sidd until you've been shown she's an impossible equation in our life.'

'Eden's angry over my walking out on her. I want you to approach her for me. Go to her and tell her how sorry I am for the way I treated her in the past, that time has proved to me she is my only true love and my life is empty without her. Explain that we both miss her and want her to be a part of our lives. Make her understand that it was her fault I had to leave her and that it was the greatest mistake of my life. What am I telling you? You're a master at getting women interested in me.'

'Things are a bit different now, Garfield. You have a wife, a son. The wife Eden wanted to be, the child you never had together. She may not want to take that problem on,' suggested Dante.

'That won't matter to Eden if you make her understand that I am in a marriage that is more of a business arrangement than a love match. That we stay together for the sake of our son and her social ambitions. Eden would love Desmond as much as I do and I would take him with me if I were to divorce Claudine.'

'I don't like it!' exclaimed Dante.

'No, but you will like the rewards. With her connections, once we are a part of Eden's life again, all sorts of doors will open for us. The galleries won't want to pass up a chance to exhibit our paintings. Think of all the socialising and the new people we'll have entrée to. You love New York and there's Eden's flat there which we can use to show our work to prospective clients. And, most important, you want to see me happy – it's a long time since I have been.'

'There are other women I can find for you, Garfield. And though one does not want be crude they're fuckable, dear boy, as fuckable as Eden, and easier to manipulate *and* surely with a great deal more money. Try and keep some perspective: she knows we have little money and yet she never, not even at the height of your fling with her, gave us a dime, never even paid our travel expenses. Big deal, she gave you a roof over your head and fed you when you were together. Don't look at me that way! We live by the generosity of wealthy men and women who appreciate that we are poor artists who need patrons to carry on with our work. You adore our houses in Hydra, Venice, this studio and our flats here in Paris. We're all right for a few months because Cecile has sold well for you but what then?'

Garfield stroked Dante's cheek, kissed him and told him, 'Do this for me. I promise she can be made a part of our extended family, and if she cannot I will leave her once and for all.'

Garfield could see the love for him in Dante's eyes and knew his friend would do it. Pimping was a way of life for them, always had been for as long as they had been together. Dante had a love for Garfield that was unshakable, he simply could not say no to him. That was what kept them together. He loved Garfield the way a woman loves a man. Garfield, even after all the years they had been together, flirted outrageously with him to get what he wanted. They were like a couple in an open marriage, truly partners in life.

Dante was eccentric in his dress; in his day-to-day living he had not a strand of moral fibre. He was avaricious yet never wasted money, a luxury-loving miser who played the role of struggling artist to the hilt. Yet he collected grand houses and lived in them in genteel poverty. He was in fact a better painter than Garfield but was lazy whereas Garfield always found the energy to work. Everything they did in life was to promote Garfield and his work. They were extremely clever hustlers.

Dante had enormous charm in a Byzantine fashion.

He was welcome wherever he wanted to be. Men and women with time and money on their hands enjoyed his company. He was enormously knowledgeable about art and fed it to his victims like pap to a baby. He created an aura around him of other worldliness as if half the time he was in a state of nirvana. The ladies who lunch and do the galleries, art dealers and successful painters, millionaire businessmen who saw him for what he was but toyed with him anyway, loved that in him.

Dante represented to them a bohemian lifestyle missing from their world. He was clever about enticing them on with something they could never have and would always want. He represented the other side of their lives, a life of no responsibilities, no morality, and he could paint whereas all they could do was buy their diversions. He made them feel he was a superior being because he could meditate and make meditation and stillness his true self. No matter how many victims he left the poorer in his wake, he could always find replacements.

Eden woke late on her first day back home. The scent of frying bacon wafted through the house, a pleasant aroma to wake up to. She slipped into a pale blue moiré robe with navy blue velvet revers and stared at herself in a full-length mirror framed in early-nineteenth-century Damascus work. She was surprised to see a beautiful face, younger than her years. There was a vitality in it that had not been there the last time she had looked in that mirror. She felt incredibly happy but a stranger to herself, her bedroom, her own house.

She looked away from the mirror to her room: the dishevelled bed, the furniture, the view through the window. They were all the same, it was merely she who was different. A strange sensation but not one to dwell on. Her life had been suspended in this house while she had played the game of getting old; now she was back there would be much to get used to in the new Eden Sidd.

The dogs! Eden flung open her bedroom door and took them by surprise. They had been lying on the floor outside. They scrambled to their feet and charged at her, nearly knocking her over. They all barked, Chekov howled, the Shi Tsus leaped high into the air. Winkie, after several tries, made it into Eden's arms. Wonkie, always competitive and looking for attention, only seconds later landed on Winkie. The pair continued to yap in between licking her face. Chekov the Russian wolfhound pressed against Eden and pushed her to the bed where she collapsed. In a flash the three dogs were there on it as well, crawling all over her.

They quite obviously saw no difference in her. She had the good grace to recognise that and laugh at herself about the change that had come over her. She made up her mind then and there that her feeling of being a new woman would remain her secret. It was too private, a very personal sensation that had nothing to do with anyone else. People would think it fanciful, dramatic at the very least.

It took a considerable time for the dogs to settle. With

Wonkie in her arms and Chekov and Winkie following on her heels she went downstairs and walked through the hall and into the kitchen.

'Scrambled or poached? They're duck eggs. Picked them up this morning,' said Rachel who had her back to Eden and now turned round.

'Fried, I think.'

'My, but you look well! You must have had a wonderful time. I'm glad to see you,' said a smiling Rachel.

Eden grabbed a piece of toast that had just popped up from the toaster. She sat down in the chair closest to her housekeeper who was cooking again.

'I have a great deal to tell you. There are going to be some changes round here.'

'Why's that?'

'Because I'm going to play in public again.'

'What kind of changes?'

Typical of Rachel to get right down to basics, thought Eden. 'Well, for one thing there'll be more people around trying to see me. I might on occasion have to see them. People will be curious about my lifestyle so we'll have to keep a low profile and stay quiet about my love affairs.'

'You've no need to worry about love affairs, I haven't seen many of them round here lately.'

'That's cheeky of you, Rachel.'

'I wish I did have something to reveal, for your sake not mine.'

Rachel poured herself a cup of coffee and sat down next to Eden. 'What are you telling me exactly?' she pressed.

Rachel was a West Country woman who had always lived a simple uncomplicated life. Eden had been living quite simply for all the years Rachel had been with her and she had no idea of the sort of fame and lifestyle her employer had been used to before she settled in Gloucestershire. Suddenly Eden's life was going to go into high gear and Rachel was more necessary than ever to her now.

'What I want to tell you is that I am going to make a comeback in the music world and that means I must work harder than ever and need to be more private than ever. I want you to run my day-to-day life, keep people at bay unless I tell you otherwise. We will probably be entertaining more, too.'

There, it was all said. There was nothing else to do for now except fit back into her English country house routine. There was a hellish amount of post to get through first. Max would be sending one of his assistants down for one or two days a week to deal with it and the telephone.

The mundane worries of life would be wiped out of Eden's world. She knew very well how to cosset herself, how to submerge herself in an existence of nothing but love and music, sex and music, which was where she wanted to be again.

For several days after her return Eden worked with the gardener, did some cooking, went through her wardrobe. These were luxuries she had been able to take as a way of life during the past ten years. Then one day she realised she was wasting her time, precious time that could and should be used for her work. Giving up the simple things, the former uncomplicated way of life, was a price she had to pay because fate had dealt her a remarkable hand. She left everything to the gardener, to Rachel, to Max, and took up her life of music and her restored sexual life.

In the ten years that she had been in semi-retirement Eden had kept most of her friends at arm's length. She kept in touch but usually by telephone or letters, isolated comfortably from her own point of view but never theirs.

Now the news was out about her comeback and Max's public relations campaign was in full gear friends were clamouring to see her. For weeks she met people she had put on the back burner of her life. Flowers to wish her well arrived nearly every day from admirers. Laurent called almost every night before he took up his baton. Soon they both began to realise that telephone sex was not enough. They agreed they should cool the sexual heat between them and find other partners to play erotic games with. If word of their telephone sex were to become public it would be ruinous for both of them, especially with the concerts they were to do together. The tabloids would make a meal of their sexual attraction for each other and they were too level-headed to allow that to happen.

Men who had formerly seen Eden as over the hill sexually now made overtures. She liked it. It made her feel quite marvellous. Suddenly she was spoiled for choice in sexual partners which amused her. It was so nice to be wanted for her sensuality. She flirted outrageously as she had done when she was young and had the pick of almost every man who crossed her path.

When the phone calls from Laurent stopped, Eden missed them. They were after all very sexy and had done wonders for her nights alone in bed. Then, after nearly a week, he called again. He missed her sexually, he said, wanted her. It was hard to say no, that they must abide by their decision to cool their ardour for each other. Even that conversation, the mere sound of lust for her in his voice, stirred her sexually. But somehow good sense prevailed on both sides and the telephone calls stopped. His occasional gifts to her did not.

Eden was taken aback by the number of people who wanted press interviews, then the radio and TV talk shows. Suddenly she was a hot property. It seemed that taking a ten-year sabbatical was the best thing she could have done to further her career. Both concerts in Epidaurus were sold out while offers from concert halls round the world were pouring in to Max's office. And always the big questions remained. What had made Eden Sidd return to the concert stage? Was she still, after such a lengthy absence, able to play with the same musical genius she had once possessed? And what about her playing the legendary Surabaya? How had she come by that? It had been out of sight in private hands for decades.

The outside world was pressing in on her but Eden paid little attention to it all. She resumed her quiet life in the English countryside, practised every day, walked the dogs and let everyone else get on with their jobs.

She did the interviews that Max deemed necessary. Having been seen out and about sporting a tantalising new look, several swains appeared and managed to persuade her into evenings out. She was an honoured guest at a dinner party hosted by a local duke, had sex with several dishy English gentlemen who were handsome, very sexy, and completely discreet.

Eden had never felt better, had not been as happy with herself as she was now for years. Suddenly she remembered how charmed a life she had once lived before Garfield, and even for a time with him. She was also playing the cello like an angel.

Chapter 14

Several weeks after Eden had returned home, she found the time to drive into the village. First she went to the cheese shop and browsed.

'Haven't seen you around for quite a while. I figured you were away. Thought we might have lost your custom until Rachel told us where you were. Greece, wasn't it?' asked the cheese lady.

Eden said as little as she could without being rude and fled from the shop. She knew how the village folk liked to know everything; frequently did in fact know everything. At other times she had found their gossiping amusing, it had become a part of living in the country. She told herself there was no particular animus in the villagers' curiosity. When she went into the butcher's shop it was more or less the same friendly inquisition. Where had she taken her holiday? Had it been one of those package deals? Mr Cobb was looking for one for him and his wife.

Actually, Mr Cobb and the cheese lady took Eden back in time. She was reminded that she may have changed but they would not necessarily know it. They were just behaving towards her as they had for the past ten years. By the time she stopped at the bakery for some cream slices, she was even prepared to volunteer the fact that she had had a marvellous time. Her old routine took over then and next she went for lunch at the Frog's Hollow tea room. She was smiling when she entered the cafe. This, after all, was where it had all started or finished, depending on how you looked at it.

The bell over the door rang as she entered. The room fell silent for a few seconds as it always did when someone entered. All eyes were upon Eden. The proprietor Grace Peebles carrying two Thursday specials for the lunching ladies Edna Archer and Beryl Pike, looked harried but pleased to see Eden. There were two middle-aged men at another table, a young couple and a pram at the table in the window. The man who had not given her a second glance several months before was sitting alone at a table close to the kitchen door.

Several people spoke to her. Beryl and Edna were their usual sweet selves. 'We've missed you. Been away?' asked Beryl.

'Yes, and it's nice to be back,' replied Eden.

'Like me, always glad to get home from a holiday no matter how different and exciting it might be there,' said Edna.

The two women were flushed with delight at talking with her again. Eden found herself really pleased to be back in Frog's Hollow, talking to Edna and Beryl who were so easy and pleasant. Suddenly conversations they had once had together came flooding back to mind and though she felt a million light years away from these two women now she made a point of not slighting them. 'Those carrots look nice, Mrs Pike. The greengrocer or the supermarket?'

There followed a dissertation on the price of carrots sold loose and those with their green tops still on. Eden then told them about the cheese and cream slices she had bought and finally took leave of them to sit at the last available table.

'You're lucky, I've got one more Thursday special left. You want it?' asked Grace as she dashed past.

'Yes,' said Eden without questioning what it was.

She was aware that the handsome stranger was unable to stop staring at her. He was looking at her in the direct way men do when they find a woman who is sexually appealing to them. Every woman recognises that special look. It brought a smile to Eden's face. She glanced in the mirror on the wall opposite her. Even she could see the difference in her looks compared to the last time she had lunched at Frog's Hollow when he had ignored her.

Eden was not a woman who primped. She had always had the kind of good looks that came naturally. She had been confident in them, knew how to dress provocatively and how to show herself off to advantage. The woman she saw in the mirror was dressed in a pair of cream-coloured wide-legged trousers that clung to her hips and fitted her bottom sensually. Her jacket was of yellow leather, short, and moulded like a second skin. Around her neck she wore a white finely pleated chiffon scarf

189

tied dramatically. Her hair was slightly dishevelled which was always a good look on Eden. However, there was something about the way the stranger was looking at her that did make her primp. She ran her fingers flirtatiously through her hair, wiped the corners of her pale-lipsticked mouth, then sat down.

Beryl and Edna were looking at her. Caught staring, one nudged the other and Edna, to cover their rudeness, said, 'It's lamb today, creamed potatoes, broccoli and carrots.'

The tea room was so small everyone heard them talking across the tables and no one thought it odd. Actually it was quite the norm. Everyone talked to everyone here. There was something strangely social about the Thursday special crowd, probably because it all began and ended in an hour.

Sam Perry said, 'There's a choice for pudding. I suggest you take the spotted dick,' directing his words towards Eden.

'I'm partial to strawberry jam so I've taken the roly-poly,' said the man lunching with Mr Perry.

By the time her meal arrived there were conversations going on across the room between all the tables. All except the handsome stranger's.

Grace Peebles arrived at Eden's table and deposited a plateful of food. She then sat down and wiped her brow with a clean tea towel she had been carrying. 'Mind a bit of company?' she asked.

'Not at all.'

'People have been asking after you. We were worried

something had happened to you. You've been away a long time. Then Mr Perry here bumped into Rachel and we heard you were away on holiday. That's so, isn't it, Sam?'

'Yes, Rachel came into the shop to have me mend your flat iron, Miss Sidd. If she hadn't done that we wouldn't have known anything about where you was.'

'I knew. I read it in the *Standard*,' said the young man rocking the pram with one hand while he forked food into his mouth with the other.

'You never said,' his wife commented.

'You never asked,' he replied.

Eden was cutting into the delicious lamb on her plate when Grace said, 'Joey Chalk, you are a one! We've got a real live lady who gets in the papers living right here amongst us and you never said a word.'

'It was something about a million-dollar fiddle.'

'Cello, not a violin,' said the stranger.

'Oh, I don't think you've met this gentleman, Eden,' said Grace. 'He's become one of our Thursday special people, haven't you, Tom?'

'Yes.'

'Eden Sidd, this is Tom Spurling. He's a photo-journalist, living over in Sutton Benjamin. Seems he's been hereabouts for years but travels for his work quite a lot. Not now, though, he's working on a book,' said Grace, sounding quite proud of her new customer.

'Hello,' said Tom Spurling and went back to his pudding.

Eden gave him a dazzling smile and said, 'How clever

of you to have found the best kept secret in the county, the Thursday special at Frog's Hollow.'

He raised his head and gazed into her eyes. 'It did take some finding but when we're travelling in strange lands the first thing we journalists look for is a decent bed, the second the best food, so habit prevailed and I found Grace and Frog's Hollow.'

Grace puffed up with pleasure. Tom Spurling had charm, knew how to flatter. Eden found him mysteriously attractive. Physically he was sexy with that aura of masculinity to which women feel instantly attracted. He had a lovely accent, too, educated but definitely northern. It made him appear a bit of a rough diamond. These deductions were made purely by instinct, though, because really he gave very little away. Eden sensed he was the sort of man who liked florist's girls, hairdressers, barmaids. Nothing complicated. He was the type who liked sex on the run with young delicious ladies, beautiful with great bodies and no complications. Or maybe older married women out for a lark with a man who would not complicate his life or theirs. And career women might excite his interest, those who were independent and had no need of support from him of any kind.

All this was going through her head while she ate and Grace chatted. When Eden was halfway through her meal she looked up at Tom Spurling to find him studying her. There was something he liked about her, that was evident.

Grace left Eden's table and she was at last able to eat

undisturbed. She enjoyed eating alone and sensed that so did the handsome newcomer. He rose from his chair then and pulled on a black leather jacket. Leaving the money for his lunch on the table, he nodded to Eden and walked from the tea room. Once he had closed the glass door, he glanced once more at her through it and smiled, putting his hand to his forehead and giving her a smart salute.

That night in bed she thought about Tom Spurling. There was something very appealing about him. She realised that her attraction to him when she had first seen him was what had made the pain of being ignored by him so acute. Well, he certainly hadn't ignored her this time. He had been openly flirting with her. Eden went to sleep with a smile on her face.

All the way home from Frog's Hollow, Tom kept thinking of Eden Sidd. He had not been so intensely attracted to a lady as he was to her for a very long time. She was a very sexy woman. Everything about her was sensual: her face, that body, the size of her breasts and bottom, the long legs that appeared to go on forever. And especially her hands with their long and slender fingers.

Of course he knew who she was, even had a recording of hers. An old girlfriend of his had given it to him one Christmas. She was undeniably a great musician, no little thing but something to put aside for now because primarily he fancied her rotten. He sensed that they would be great together in bed. He had a passion not only to fuck her breathless but to make love to her.

There had been very few women in Tom's life whom he'd wanted to love, give himself over to with no holds barred, but today he'd found one. It had been an instantaneous desire that was so powerful he'd had to run away from Eden just to get himself in balance. He had never felt this way about any other woman. Her mere presence was so powerful, so rich. She'd shone in that simple place like a star, sounding like a goddess come to earth when she had talked carrots and cheese with the two old dears. She had such class, such style, saying nothing when the young father had called the glorious Surabaya a 'fiddle'. Had Tom not spoken up, he was sure she would never even have corrected the young man.

He sat in his kitchen in a rocking chair, trying to force her out of his mind. Eden Sidd was not the type of woman to get involved with. She was years older than he, terrifyingly clever and talented, with a whole celebrity life going for her. Tom himself had a penchant for dusky charmers, ladies of the night, hot sex and hotter women, good time girls who understood that his lifestyle was one of here today and gone tomorrow. He had always been an adventurer, a man who took chances every day for his work. He had covered several African wars and many more tragedies. His colleagues and competitors had nicknamed him Kamikaze Tom.

Now he was fed up with war, had had enough death and destruction, poverty, starvation, maiming, blood and guts to last him a lifetime. That was what his book was about, a reportage of his years of photographing the dark side, the meanness, the evil in life. After its completion he intended to photograph only the beautiful and sublime, facets of nature still untouched by man.

Tom had not so much lost his nerve for danger as burned himself out. He wanted the lighter side of life and though he had not been looking for a woman, there was something so positive and right about Eden Sidd he actually thought he would die without her. Dramatic in the extreme but that was the way he felt.

The feeling was so intense and out of the ordinary that he had not the least idea of how to cope with it. Eden Sidd drew him to her like a magnet. He had to find a way to become close to her. What madness! For all he knew she might be married, in love with a man, have children. He knew nothing about her except that he had found his soulmate, someone with whom to build a life, the sort of life that he had so far missed. This was the woman he wanted to grow old with.

His cottage was by a trout stream, isolated but within walking distance of a village. He went down to the river for some fly fishing. The peace and tranquillity of the slow-running river calmed him somewhat. He cast his line time after time and the sound of the river, the early-spring sunshine, the scent of the wood and wild flowers, did their work. He regained some of the balance he had lost when he'd fallen in love with Eden. He would bring her here fishing, he decided. Teach her the ways of the river, how the trout ran. She was already a part of his life.

That evening he went to a pub, drank much too much

and chatted up a young thing: blonde, blue-eyed, quite sweet and silly. He took her home, feeling incredibly sexy, wanting to fuck into oblivion this pretty young thing who worked at the supermarket. She came, many times, ending up by begging him to come but no matter how they fucked he couldn't. He stayed rigid and full of desire, not for the young girl but for Eden.

It seemed to Tom that the following Thursday would never come. The days dragged by. It was difficult to focus on his work. Every hour he was away from Eden he kept promising himself he would do something about meeting her. She had an unlisted number, he had checked that, going through his contacts book for anyone who might be able to help. He used up many favours but Tom was not a successful world-class photojournalist for nothing. If he had managed to get the likes of Gadafi and Mubarak to sit for him and be interviewed with hard and sharp questions, he certainly had the clout to get Eden's private number.

He deduced rightly that no one in Frog's Hollow would have it. He rarely stopped in Frog's Hollow for morning coffee and certainly never for afternoon tea. But he did now and Grace sat down with him and offered some information. 'Is it true, do you think, that Eden plays a musical instrument worth a million dollars?'

'Probably more,' Tom answered, trying to appear disinterested.

'She's such a nice simple woman, so down to earth. She'll speak to anyone.'

'Not so simple, I think, Grace. Simple uncomplicated

women do not play a cello worth in excess of a million dollars, and especially one that has been given to them as a gift. And they don't make a triumphal return to the serious music world in an ancient Greek amphitheatre.'

'Fiddle, cello, violin . . . what do I know about those sort of instruments? What I *do* know about is money. A million dollars! Imagine, she knows people who give away gifts like that. A woman who's happy with my Thursday specials.'

'What's her husband like?' asked Tom, trying to sound as casual as he could.

'Far as I know she doesn't have one. And not looking either,' said Grace.

'How do you know that?'

'Because she's never seen out and about. Very anti-social except when she occasionally goes to one of the Duke's dinners. Someone said she played at a private party for Prince Charles there, but that might be just gossip so don't quote me. Oh, I'm sure she has men, though. A woman like that – all she'd have to do was whistle. Remember when Lauren Bacall said that to Humphrey Bogart?'

Grace leaned towards Tom and punched him playfully in the chest. 'You planning to pucker up and blow, Tom?' she said, laughing as she left him to wait on a customer.

He called after her, 'I might just do that, Grace,' and hoped she took it as a joke.

Chapter 15

The following Thursday Eden went back to Frog's Hollow. She was early and felt disappointed to see that her handsome stranger was not there. She took the table that gave her the best view of the door. Every time the bell tinkled she raised her head to see if it was him.

There was the usual conversation between Edna, Beryl and Eden. This week it was about the price of new potatoes, Jersey Royals. Eden could not get into it, her mind too preoccupied with her versions of the Lalo Cello Concerto and Richard Strauss's 'Don Quixote', and having to go to London to see Laurent and finalise the programme for Epidaurus. The meeting was to be held in Heathrow's VIP lounge. Max had arranged it there because Laurent had a stopover of three hours before his flight on to Buenos Aires. Then she was to be a guest of the Director of Covent Garden at a gala performance of *Swan Lake*, with the newest Russian ballet wonder performing for the first time in the West. Where did Jersey Royals come into all this? she wondered, yet did not want to offend her two old friends.

She heard Edna say, 'I never buy them, they're always too expensive for me. But if you want to have some, Eden, this is the time to splurge. They're at their best.'

'Actually I'm not shopping much these days. I'm too busy working.'

'You gonna give a concert?' asked Beryl.

'Two actually.'

'Will they be on the telly?' asked Edna.

'Yes.'

'You will let us know the dates?'

'Of course.'

'Well, I can see why you haven't time to go food shopping,' conceded Beryl.

Another tinkle of the bell above the door. Eden looked up. Still not her handsome stranger. She was disappointed. Time was running out. He wasn't coming. She had been certain he would. Had been looking forward to seeing him again. She wondered whether she had been wrong. Maybe he had not been flirting with her last time. Eden told herself of course he had been. That smart salute had been a dead giveaway, that and the teasing smile that went with it.

She was tempted to ask Grace if he had been in and gone. It was possible, she told herself, that he had come early and assumed she was not going to be there. This is ridiculous, she told herself, I'm behaving like a young girl with her first crush.

'It's roast chicken today, done in tons of butter and free-range at that, roast potatoes and cauliflower cheese.'

'That'll do me just fine, thanks, Grace.'

Eden finished her meal and left the restaurant. He obviously wasn't coming. He knew very well what time to be there to get the Thursday special and hadn't turned up.

Eden conjured up his good looks, the sexy way he had about him. She was more than disappointed, having sensed something wonderful could happen between them and not just something sexual. There had been a need for her in his eyes. She could see pain behind the twinkle for her he had in them. By the time she arrived home, she had talked him back into her soul, this stranger who had already changed her life once and did not even know it. She could not think of him as Tom Spurling, not yet anyway. For her he was a romantic stranger. What to do next? she asked herself. Go back next Thursday. That was about all she could do. She was sure he would come after her when he could.

Eden practised all afternoon and then took a nap. She fell into a deep sleep dreaming of her handsome stranger and was furious when the ringing telephone woke her up. She remained lying in bed, trying to remember the dream, but could not. It had escaped her. All she could remember was the sensation of feeling happy. The telephone did not stop ringing. Finally she reached over and picked up the receiver. Seconds before she spoke she sensed it was her handsome stranger. She smiled and said, 'Hello.'

Tom Spurling hesitated before speaking. Eden's voice enchanted him. It was an intimate sound, a bedroom voice. Soft but at the same time husky, firm, decisive.

'I like your voice,' he told her.

'Is this Tom Spurling?'

'You're not offended that I've called? I don't mean to be intrusive but I missed you at the tea room and frankly can't bear to wait another week before making contact.'

'How did you get my telephone number?'

He was relieved not to hear any annoyance in her question. 'Not easily.'

'But journalists have their ways, is that it?'

Tom liked the lilt of amusement in her voice and was relieved that she had not been offended by his call. 'I would like to see you again, to talk to you. As much as I like Frog's Hollow, I think I can do better than that, somewhere quieter. I know a pub close to my cottage. You could come and see my place and then we could walk along the river to the Trout.'

Eden was given instructions as to how to get to Tom's house. She thought it was unusual that he didn't offer to pick her up, but then sensed there would be many unusual facets to Tom Spurling. Eden rarely went out at night and when she did it was usually with someone who would pick her up and drive her home. She was uneasy about being alone after dark on roads and lanes she was unfamiliar with even though she had a mobile telephone, which she never used. The dogs seemed the best choice of companion. They liked riding in the car, day or night.

What to wear to a pub? Nothing flashy, she decided, but something pretty and sexy. Youthful. Eden flung on and off half a dozen things. Nothing looked right. The bed was soon littered with clothes and time was flashing by. At last she selected the same outfit she had worn the day she had first met him. Now she was late so rushed down the stairs, the dogs at her heels, and was out and at the car door, urging the dogs into the back seat. There was the usual ten minutes of pandemonium as fur flew and the animals vied for supremacy amidst much barking and yelping.

Eden drove all the way with the map light on to follow the directions Tom had given her. The dogs settled, wrapped around each other, and she could hear Winkie and Wonkie snoring. A thirty-minute drive and she was at the edge of Tom's village and driving down an unsurfaced track through a wood. Eden was relieved she had decided on taking the dogs with her. This place seemed to be at the back of beyond. Three-quarters of a mile down the track, she saw lights and a cottage.

She stopped the car. Not a sound from the back seat. 'Some protection you are,' she said to the three dogs.

'I'll protect you,' she heard Tom say through the open window of the car. 'That is, if you think you need protection.'

'I always think I need protection. Whether it's true or not.'

Tom opened the car door and Winkie and Wonkie leapt out followed by the Russian wolfhound who was all over Tom. 'I think I'm the one who needs protection,' he told her laughingly.

The dogs ran off round the front of the cottage and Tom slipped an arm around Eden's shoulders. Like that, they walked together up a pebbled path to the entrance of his cottage. 'I was worried you weren't going to come.'

'Would you have been very disappointed?' she asked.

'Shocked more like.'

'Shocked? I don't think I understand. Why shocked?'

'It would have been the beginning of the end of my life. You see, I think I want to spend the rest of my days with you. So if you hadn't come, I might have died.'

'You've never even kissed me, how do you even know we're compatible?'

'Do you know that we're not?'

'No, actually, I know that we are,' Eden told him and stepped closer. She folded Tom's arms around her and kissed him, licking his lips with the point of her tongue. He drew deeply on her kiss and something wondrous happened to them. It was a warmth that flooded their bodies and their souls. They were liquid fire playing with ice, two melting people re-forming as one whole and complete human being. It was instant passion and togetherness, a mutual need to love each other and make love to each other.

Tom gently unfolded himself from Eden's arms. He stroked her hair, removed her pleated scarf and held it, sniffing the scent of her upon it. He unzipped her yellow leather jacket and removed it from her shoulders, dropping it to the floor. 'I want to know you, every part of you, intimately. I want to take you to the outer limits of love and lust and beyond. You are everything in the world that is lovely and I want us to be together forever.'

'I feel the same about you, Tom. Crazy as it seems, I

believe we have no time to waste. We must do nothing now, just be. Does that make any sense?'

'All the sense in the world,' he replied.

They were holding hands, gazing into each other's eyes. 'I was overwhelmed by you the minute I saw you for the first time last week,' he told her as he walked her through the sitting room of his cottage.

Together they sat down on a wolfskin blanket covering a bed set in one corner of the large room. Slowly they undressed each other and for the first time feasted on what each of them was seeing. They caressed each other, took their time learning about each other's bodies.

The lust was there, stronger than anything either of them had ever had with previous partners. They expressed that to each other, talked about it, and Tom said, 'I don't want us to get this wrong. Maybe it's not so much that what we feel for each other sexually is stronger than with other partners, so much as it's different. Something we cannot put into words, actually something that needs no comparisons. Tell me you understand that we are together for always? We are going to have the best adventure with each other all the rest of our lives.'

Eden didn't answer him. She was distracted by his naked flesh, the tone and muscle of his body, the large and erect phallus. She wanted to give herself to this man, to please him with her sexuality, to give him the pleasures he had been looking for all his life. They had kissed each other's bodies and souls for what seemed like forever and now Eden wanted to take possession of him and he to take possession of her. She sat astride

Tom and slowly fed his penis into her cunt while he sucked on her nipples and caressed her breasts. Wholly impaled upon Tom she came after she had slipped on and off him several dozen times. Then, after lying in her arms for a considerable time, he took command of fucking her into orgasm after orgasm.

Together they watched the dawn rise. How or when the dogs had found their way into the cottage Tom had no idea but they were there fast asleep lying on the floor at the foot of the bed. He kissed Eden awake and then they lay on their sides facing each other, stroking each other lovingly, having sex.

Eden wanted to say something about his having already had an impact on her life. That she had been invisible to him and been horrified by the experience. That he had in a sense saved her life and she was indebted to him. That she had not realised until now she had wanted him even then. That she had been devastated because he never gave her a second glance. She couldn't do it and realised she never would.

It was only in the dawn light that Eden really had a chance to study the room. It could not have been any other man's. It was a turn-of-the-century fishing lodge with the river very nearly at the porch. Everywhere she looked there were books piled high on tables or spilling out of bookcases. Several stuffed and mounted fish adorned the walls, and old and new framed photographs were hung in a haphazard fashion. Fishing rods leaned against walls or in the corners of the room; a fishing net with a long handle was draped over a low easy chair of worn leather. There were half-unpacked boxes and suitcases everywhere that made it look as if Tom was just settling in or else getting ready to leave. There was a large double desk with a computer on it and stacks of photographs piled neatly in row after row.

'It's bit of a mess. I confess to not being very neat but then I didn't expect to fall in love. I'm not out to impress you. You get what you see. That's the way it will have to be with me.'

'And me,' answered Eden.

'I suppose the best way to get to know each other would be to take things as they come?'

'Yes, and be able to ask each other anything we want.'

'Sort of a truth game?'

'Well, something like that.'

'I'll go first,' suggested Tom as he fried eggs for their breakfast standing naked at the cooker.

Eden, wrapped in wolfskins, sat on the worktop next to him. She crossed her legs and Tom pushed aside the skins so he could have a better view of her long shapely limbs. He smiled at her and she knew he was yet again excited by her mere presence. There was no hesitation in his eyes, he wanted her again in a carnal fashion.

'The truth is you're hungry but you'd rather fuck me again than eat,' said Eden teasingly.

'That's true. You win,' he told her as he turned the gas off and swept her from the worktop to the floor. He tore away her furs and they fucked in the kitchen while shooing the dogs away. Concentration was hampered by their laughter as the dogs constantly vied for Eden's attention.

Once more replete with their sexual escapades and feeling love and companionship towards each other, they lay silently in each other's arms. It was Tom who broke the silence, 'Is there any great love in your life I will have to duel with – pistols at ten paces and all that?'

'No, not necessary. No pistols or swords. It was a very great love but over more than ten years ago.'

'Are you sure of that?'

'One never quite forgets great loves, one always has a memory of them, but that's all.'

'I can handle that,' said Tom.

To herself Eden thought, No, my dear, you're not evil enough to cope with Garfield. But all she did say was, 'There is a man in my life – Max, my agent. He's devoted to me and we love each other very much but never in a carnal way. He's my best friend and so will always be in our life. You'll like him, I'm sure. He loves me and is as much a part of my career as I am and always will be.'

Before she could say anything more Tom told her, 'You know, I will never come between you and your music. I don't pretend to understand very much about your world but you can teach me to appreciate music – the nuances only a great artist such as you understands. Music has always been one of the things I never found enough time for but wanted to escape to. I love it and I'm bound to it but have never been able to indulge myself fully. I was always busy covering wars and pestilence, bringing them to the world through newspapers and TV.

'I had talked myself into believing I was doing something for mankind by bringing the horrors of war in front of people's eyes. Now I believe I would have done better learning to blow a trumpet or master the oboe. Forcing the world to look at my stunning black and white photographs of violence and mayhem has been my life since I left Cambridge. I may have made some people more aware, or maybe not even that. More likely smug, sad for the victims but thrilled that they themselves have been clever enough to escape another man's fate. I have seen enough violence: Somalia, Ethiopia, the massacres in Rwanda, tribal wars in Angola. Enough horrors to have burned myself out of believing the world has to know. The world does know and so what?

'You understand about fame and fortune, the other side of great talent, and so do I. I have a reputation as one of the best photojournalists working, I will always be that. I'll continue with my work but change my subjects. I will never cover another war.'

Tom stopped speaking. Eden realised his hands were trembling and that there was a nervous tremor in his voice. He had indeed seen too much of the hatred mankind can give way to in the name of freedom. She knew at that moment she had found the man who truly needed her to love him, show him the beauty and rapture she had known all her life. She leaned across him and kissed him tenderly.

'I didn't mean to go on so, but it's best that you know what has happened to me. You won't run away from a broken man, will you? Because in a way I am a broken human being, a nervous wreck of a man who wants peace and tranquillity, to make love, have lots of great and adventurous sex with you. For us to work and play together for the thrill of adventure, the fun that is still out there for the taking.'

'I don't see you as a broken man, just one who wants to change his life. And I have to tell you something that I'd thought I would keep from you. Now, having listened to you, I think it only fair you hear what I have to say about changing one's life.'

And Eden related exactly what had happened to her when Tom had not even seen her that fateful day she realised she had become invisible, one of the faceless women of a certain age who are bypassed by a handsome sensual man.

Tom was astonished by the story. How had this happened when now they were obvious soulmates? How wonderful that they should nevertheless have come together for a second shot at life. He was filled with admiration for Eden, for her refusal to lie down and be overlooked. Of course he had not seen her that day, there was nothing for him to see. A terrifying thought that any woman should be invisible to a man, that anyone should lose herself so completely. What courage, what strength, Eden had shown to escape that fate. He loved her all the more for it.

Chapter 16

Overnight Eden felt a difference in her life. She had met a man who loved her. She was in love with a man. This had happened before in her life, many times, and the love affair had always run its course. But she somehow knew this love would never run its course, would never lie down and die. How does a woman just know that? Eden did. They would marry and live together, for better or for worse, in sickness or in health.

Food was found for the dogs and eventually Tom did finish making breakfast. They were ravenous and ate with gusto. Then Eden called Rachel to say that she and the dogs would be in later.

As soon as she'd finished her conversation with her housekeeper, she turned to Tom and said, 'I am on a strict work schedule and must stay on it if I am to be ready for my concerts at Epidaurus.'

'I can live with that. I don't expect you to give up anything for me. We should never have to give up anything for each other, just let our lives flow together. I'll work when you are working. We'll play when we can and want to, and we'll have sex when the desire is there. I may not be saying it very well but you get the drift: we're not joined at the hip but free to have a life of our own and one together.'

'The thing is, when we need one other we'll be there. Lives apart as Eden Sidd and Tom Spurling, and another together.' What a lovely way to live, thought Eden.

'Would you like to learn to fish? I love my fishing – that's why I bought this lodge. I have a mile of the river on both sides of it. I'll teach you, if you like? We can spend lazy days on the river and have long lovely picnics.'

'Can we travel?' asked Eden.

'Anywhere you want to go.'

'I always take my cello,' she told him.

'I always take my cameras. When shall we get married?' he asked.

'Is that a question or a proposal?'

'I suppose it's both. I hadn't thought about it as having to be romantic, down on one knee and all that. We have, after all, known each other for no time at all. I promise to get romantic after we're married and for the rest of our lives. I'll be quite used to the idea by then. It's not a good one but, yes, it is a proposal of marriage. Please say yes, we can work out the details later.'

'This is madness but yes, I accept, and I'll hold you to your terms. Romance for the rest of our lives.'

They agreed to share their houses in England, Tom's cottage to be used mostly as a studio and for fishing, Eden's house for her work and for when they wanted to be together there. As they talked about serious things like where to live what became evident was that it didn't matter. All they really wanted was to be a part of each other's life.

Both of them had prior commitments, agents to be seen, social events to attend, and they decided they did not want to drag each other along to these engagements. They wanted for a while to be together very privately and so agreed to marry quietly and keep it a secret until they were ready to make it public on their own terms.

Eden told Tom she would like to be married in a quiet ceremony in the Greek Orthox church in Hydra where she had a house.

'The invisible net. I know Hydra very well. Always said I would marry there in the very church you suggest. I once lived there for six months while recuperating from covering the civil war in the Sudan. When would you like to go?'

'It will take some time to organise it, the red tape will be daunting.'

'No, it won't. The Patriarch owes me big time for an article and help in Cyprus. The priest in Hydra will be most discreet if I make him promise to be. You may not have had a romantic proposal but I can guarantee you a romantic and private wedding.'

Tom looked so excited, so full of passion over the idea that they were to be bound together even further. Suddenly she felt that everything she had ever done in her life, everything she'd loved, had been a necessary step towards arriving here at this time in her life, with this man and no other.

That very day they moved into each other's lives and houses. Rachel looked shocked but happy to have a man around the house and in Eden's life. She was sworn to secrecy, told she must not gossip about the event because they wanted privacy, they would tell her when they were ready to go public.

Rachel saw it as very romantic, very glamorous, and Tom eased into the household without a problem. They decided Eden would tell Max as soon as the right opportunity came along. He would give her away at the wedding.

They had been together for two weeks when Eden had to attend the meeting at Heathrow with Max and Laurent and was going on from there to the ballet. Max's car was sent for her while Tom went to Bath to meet an old colleague.

Life seemed suddenly empty without him at her side. There was a rightness about Tom's and Eden's being together that made her feel there had always been something wrong with every other man until now. Was it any wonder that previous love affairs wore themselves out? It was quite simple. She had never, until Tom, met the right man, had only thought she had.

Max was waiting at the terminal for her. They went directly to the VIP lounge where Laurent was waiting. He was pacing the floor and seemed nervous. It occurred to her that this was the first time they would have met each other since Alexandria. Max and Laurent's travelling companion, his personal assistant, tried to orchestrate the meeting but Laurent was not having it. He left them talking together and walked Eden over to a pair of chairs in a corner of the room, called a steward and ordered a bottle of champagne.

His first words to her were, 'You look ravishing. I must talk with you privately. Don't look askance. No scenes, I promise.'

'Laurent, what's this all about? You're frightening me. Has something happened? You can't do the concert? You want me to change the programme?'

'No. Something has happened but it has nothing do with the concerts or the programme. Max is doing us both proud in the manner in which he is organising things. This has to do with us, my dear. You and me.'

The look of relief on Eden's face brought Laurent to a halt. He seemed more in control now, calmer about whatever was on his mind. He kissed Eden's hand, stroked her cheek. She could see the lust for her in his eyes but also something else, something she could not understand.

'Ever the professional, I admire you for that. I always have. The look of relief on your face! Music always did come before me, even when we were together. I can't blame you for that, I'm like it now myself.'

An ice bucket arrived and Laurent dismissed the steward, opened the wine and poured two glasses. He handed one to Eden. 'To Epidaurus and a night to remember all the days of our lives,' was the toast he graciously gave.

'I will always love you, Eden. I imagine I will never stop wanting you sexually. The erotic world I have had with you has never been bettered by another woman and never will. I learned in Alexandria that you will always love me in that way too. But those telephone calls afterwards were becoming a sexual dependency neither of us was satisfied with. They were turning into sick sex, something neither of us deserves to be left with.

'I didn't want you to hear this from anyone else but me. I have found someone else to love, someone who will love me as you never could. She looks at me in that same way you used to look at Garfield. The way you never have and never will look at me. I can't waste my life waiting for you to give me what I want, whereas I can get it from Francine. She is young, beautiful, and I am going to be happy with her. Make her the mother of my children, the woman of my life. Don't be upset. We can make marvellous music together, be friends, always feel carnal love for each other in a make-believe world. Fuck each other in our dreams and our fantasies. And there is always Max for you. Put him out of his misery and make a life with him. You'll not do better.

'I know that you love me the best way you can and have always done so. And we will always have Alexandria, a lasting memory, one that will not be easy to forget. I'm sorry to let you down like this but I have moved on. Don't be hurt and angry that our love has run its course. I think you told me that same thing more than once. It hurt me so much then. It will take time but one day you too will forgive and may even find someone to replace me.

'You haven't said anything. Is there nothing you want to say to me?' asked Laurent.

Eden could not think of a single thing to say that would not offend him. What, after all, could she say? 'You vain, pompous prick! How dare you presume to know about my feelings for you or any other man? Fix me up with Max? We will always have Alexandria . . . a lasting memory that will not be easy to forget? It was forgotten in a flash the moment Tom Spurling declared he loved me.'

The difference between Laurent and Tom was huge. There was no contest there. One was the man she had been looking for all her life while the other was just a man. But there really was no point at all in talking to Laurent or telling him she had finally found the man she wanted to marry and grow old with.

The kindest thing she could do was not to steal his thunder. Let him believe that he was dropping her and she was, as he wanted to believe, devastated by losing him. Laurent needed the satisfaction that goes with deliberately hurting someone, a saving face sort of thing on his part, the ploy of a little man. Well, she had always been a bigger person than he, this was no time to bring herself down to his level.

'So this Francine is the reason you no longer needed to go on with our erotic phone calls, that we have not been together since Alexandria? Wife, the mother of your children, young and beautiful . . . everything I am not. How cruel to remind me of the things I lack. You expect friendship to compensate for losing you? Is that what this is all about?' asked Eden, playing to his vanity.

'That's all I am prepared to give you. Isn't it enough?' was his reply.

'I guess it will have to be. We are two civilised people and it seems to me friendship is no little thing. At least I heard this news from you and that's something. Give me time, I'll get over you.'

Eden watched him closely and was amazed at the vanity of men. The look of self-satisfaction, the sense of one-upmanship in the love stakes, was written all over his face. A brilliant conductor with a knowledge of music that was sublime felt the need to feed his own vanity, believing a few inches of sexual organ gave him absolute power to wield over her. Was it any wonder their love affair had run its course?

Eden wanted to put Laurent in his place and tell him, 'Too late, I have found Mr Right and Mr Right has found me.' But what was the point? Why alienate someone who would be a good friend? Why embarrass him, spoil the game he was playing? Soon enough he would meet Tom. Then Laurent would open his eyes and see how happy Eden was, no longer blinded by his own vanity.

They finished the bottle of champagne and talked briefly about the upcoming concert. Then his flight was called and Laurent kissed Eden deeply, sensually. He caressed her face, held her close to his body until she could feel his sex straining against his trousers. He whispered loving sensual words and licked and kissed her ear lobe. Gently she pushed him away. She had played along with his game but this was overplaying his hand. 'This must end, never again, you have Francine now,' she said, walking away.

In the car on the way to Covent Garden and the ballet Eden nearly told Max about Tom and their plans to wed. What stopped her was the idea of the outside world sharing what they had together, even someone as close to her as Max. It was too much of an intrusion on their very private world.

Max noticed that she was pensive and asked her, 'Did Laurent upset you about something?'

'No, quite the contrary though he thinks he has. It's too tedious to get into. Laurent is still a little boy in many ways.'

'He always will be. That's part of his charm. It's why you left him for Garfield. He will always be a child prodigy even when he's an old man. He will never quite grow up.'

'That's astute of you, Max. But then you always are.'

He took her hand and squeezed it in the dark. 'You seem somehow happier, more content with your life. There is something more to this than the concerts.'

'Yes, there is something. I have a secret, one I would like to hold on to for a little while longer. Grant me that?' she asked, and leaned against him to give him a kiss on the cheek.

Max was on to her. He knew her better than anyone. The Eden Sidd charm, the sensual little ways that always worked on him. He would not pry or cajole her into revealing her secret. That had never been the way with them. They never manipulated each other, were always straight and honest in their dealings.

Street lights were flashing past the car as they sped along the Cromwell Road on their way to the West End. Now it was Eden's turn. She felt that Max was being reserved about something. He too had a secret, one he thought she was best not knowing. They went down Exhibition Road and into Hyde Park. The traffic was heavy but they were still moving.

'There will be a crush of people going to this Gala. It's the hottest ticket in town, everyone wants one. The loathsome Dante actually called asking me to get a pair of seats for Garfield and him. Not a word for ten years and then he tries to hustle seats from me!'

So that was Max's news. Eden felt her blood run cold. If Dante wanted seats at the ballet he would get seats. Why call Max, though? They detested each other. It must be that Dante wanted Eden to know they were in town or he would never have called. That devious Byzantine mind. Dante and Garfield . . . her life and love with Tom were miles away from that nasty gigolo and his pimp. Not even bad news could mar her evening, though. Eden laughed aloud and told Max, 'Dante's a worm, not worth thinking about.'

He knew that she meant that and breathed a sigh of relief. Their car drew up before the Opera House and Eden slipped out, Max having jumped out first to help her. His eyes scanned the crowd moving into the house. Eden looked extremely glamorous dressed in a long black gown that hugged her figure and wrapped in a diaphanous shawl of plum-coloured silk as fine as a spider's web. Neither of them saw Dante lingering in the crowd, watching.

Eden and Max entered their box and were greeted by the Director of Covent Garden. They were introduced to several other guests and given a glass of champagne and tiny smoked salmon sandwiches. Eden was shown to a chair at the front of the box next to a man in black tie, his head buried in an evening newspaper. A smiling Max removed the newspaper from his hands just as the house lights dimmed. 'I believe you know this man or so he says.'

'Tom Spurling at your service, ma'am.' And he raised Eden's hand and pressed a kiss upon her fingers.

Chapter 17

The Russian wonder was indeed a wonder. He left his audience breathless with excitement. Another Nureyev, a taller Baryshnikov. Names of great male dancers of the past were on everyone's lips. There were heart-stopping leaps, magnificent *pas de deuxs*. Filled with joy and wonder, the audience delivered a ten-minute standing ovation.

All through the evening Eden wanted to know how Tom had pulled off his coup. But there was no time, the dancer held them all enthralled. Afterwards there was a supper which Eden and Tom skipped out on. Max covered for them with an acceptable excuse. Tom had other plans. In Max's car they sat in the back seat while his driver threaded through the traffic and they managed to get out of Covent Garden.

'Alone at last! Now one of you had better tell me how you managed this magnificent surprise. I want to hear it all, every detail,' Eden told them.

'You begin, Max,' said Tom.

'From the beginning?' he asked.

'Yes, no secrets, from the very beginning.'

'You both look so smug and sound like a double act. Do get on with it, Max,' prompted Eden.

'About a week ago I had a phone call from Tom. Of course, I knew his name. He asked me to lunch.'

'What do you mean, he asked you to lunch? Just like that, out of the blue, and you accepted? That sounds very strange to me.'

'Are you going to keep interrupting?' Max scolded.

'Sorry.'

'As I was saying, I had this phone call from Tom who got past my secretary by mentioning he was a friend of an old friend of mine, Jason Wildeman, a journalist who had been very good to us in the past. I tried to get out of lunch but Tom hooked me in when he said, "This is about Eden Sidd."

'We arranged to meet at the Foreign Corespondents' Club. At the bar we had a few drinks and he came directly to the point. I think you should pick it up from there, Tom.'

Eden was intrigued. She was also aware that Max liked Tom, so they must have got on right from the beginning. She said nothing but waited for Tom to take over, very much in the dark about why he went to meet Max.

'I called on Max because I knew how important he was to your life and would be to mine. I am deeply in love with you, Eden, and found it increasingly difficult to keep that a secret, especially from someone as important as Max is to you. I suppose it was a man thing. Having to see what I have to contend with. If Max and I get on all our lives will be easier. The object of the exercise was to meet the competition.

'I liked the look of Max the very first time I saw him waiting at the bar. I went up to him and told him, "Thank you for seeing me. There is no mystery here and I don't want there to be any." We shook hands and he said, "You mentioned Eden Sidd?" "Yes, I'm going to marry her and I thought you should know that as you're so much a part of her life," I said.

'He took an enormous swallow of Scotch and then asked me, "Don't you think Eden should be the one to tell me such important news?" "Oh, she plans to," I told him. "But, you see, I wanted to make sure that you and I liked each other first. I had to know who I'm dealing with. Not from Eden, who would be biased, but from instinct, yours and mine. I need you to know that I do not take my love for Eden lightly, nor her career, and neither do I want to hinder in any way the relationship you have together. I felt that if I waited for Eden to take the initiative and tell you in a few weeks' times there would already be a breach in our relationship, a secret, that would put you off base. It would be harder to get to know you. That's not what I want."

'Of course the next problem was, how was I going to tell you that I had gone behind your back to meet Max? After he'd checked me out with Jason Wildeman, he called me and we had a second lunch. Jason had assured Max that if I had declared myself in any way then I would deliver the goods. "A man of honour", was how he put it. Yes, that was it, he called me a man of honour.

'It was my idea that we bring it all out in the open as soon as possible – that is, between the three of us. I was insistent that we should keep it from the public a little while longer out of pure selfishness on our part, enjoying the privacy and all that.

'To surprise you was my idea. How, when and where was Max's.'

Eden leaned over and kissed Tom then turned towards Max and told him, 'I will always love you but never as much as I do now for immediately recognising that Tom is the right man for me. For us.' Then she kissed Max and she and Tom said goodbye.

A few minutes later they were in front of a small French restaurant on Charlotte Street. The glitter and glitz of the earlier part of the evening was left behind in Covent Garden. Chez Jean-Pierre had only seven tables covered in blue and white checked tablecloths, a red candle aglow in a silver candleholder on each. It was smoky and smelled of heavenly French cuisine. All the tables were taken save for one.

Eden and Tom entered the restaurant and were greeted effusively by the chef's wife, Ann-Marie. Tom introduced Eden to her and they were shown to their table.

Eden's first impression was that it was one of those charming out-of-the-way little bistros one finds everywhere in France. Typical of the sort of place Tom would seek out. Great food, no pretensions, inexpensive. In fact, however, it was more like a private dining club.

One did not just walk in off the street, the tables were always reserved, and the menu was extraordinary. One did not choose. The chef cooked what he wanted and everyone wanted what Jean-Pierre cooked.

First of all tall flutes of champagne arrived. There was a continual amazing contrast here between simplicity and elegance, the rough and the smooth. It was an atmosphere so special it took Eden by surprise. She had no preconceived ideas about what this man she had fallen in love with was like. He was full of surprises: approaching Max as he had, turning up at the ballet as he did, and now the first place he took her was something unique. He was definitely every bit the adventure he had promised to be when he'd asked Eden to marry him and she was enthralled.

'However did you discover this place?' she asked as plates of whole foie gras were placed in front of them and fresh glasses of perfect Sauternes to go with it. Miniature brioches were served with the goose liver.

'I used to dine at their restaurant in Algeria. They had a terrible time resettling and so a few friends and I helped them to get going by forming a dining club. Pure selfishness. I told you, journalists always seek out the best place to eat and the best place to sleep.'

Eden sensed there was much more to the story than that but did not press the subject. She had learned a useful lesson about her life to be with Tom Spurling. They were going to let things unfold slowly, the best way to get to know and love each other even better.

During the next few hours they dined as grandly as if

they had been to the best four-star restaurant in Lyon or Paris. The bill was astronomical. Tom paid with a credit card and caught her gazing at the cost.

He smiled and said, 'I suppose married people do talk about money. Are you perhaps wondering if I can afford to keep us in the style to which you are accustomed? The answer is, I don't know on two counts: first, I don't know how you live so we will have to see. Second: I have put away most of my earnings and lived on my expense account for close to twenty years. The money is invested and all I have bought for years is the fishing lodge and some land round it. When I gave up warmongering I spoke to the accountant to see if I could afford to change my work. War and pestilence is lucrative, pretty pictures may not be. He told me, "Change your life, Tom, you can afford it. You have a portfolio worth eight million US dollars." We're wealthy, Eden. Wealthy beyond my imagination. Enough to do whatever we want for as long as we choose.'

'You mean to support me?'

'Why sound so surprised?'

'I have money from my work.'

'Good, then we have that much more to play with, but the important thing is, it's yours, it's mine, it's ours. Who cares whose it is? All that matters is that we can afford to get married.'

Eden realised that she had fallen in love with an innocent, someone who could never imagine the devious ins and outs that can occur in love. At last she had met someone selfless who loved her. She could not but think of Garfield, all the love she had invested in him and how he had manipulated her. It was like the Black Knight coming up against the White. A shiver ran down her spine. She had spent years loving the Black Knight, playing on the dark side of the moon.

'Are you chilly?' asked Tom.

'No.'

'I thought I saw you shiver,' he insisted.

'Just someone walking over my grave,' Eden told him.

'I suppose we have to expect that. Great loves die hard, and sometimes not at all,' said Tom, and changed the subject.

Eden picked up immediately that he was no fool. He was aware that she had a past and it didn't matter to him. He was secure enough about them as a couple to accept her past loves and let her deal with them.

The evening was perfect. As Tom had promised, if his proposal of marriage had not been romantic, their future would be. From the restaurant they drove to the fishing lodge in his old battered Honda. Dawn was just coming up and there was a mist on the river. Neither of them much felt like sleep, so Tom lit the fire and Eden made tea. They lay in front of the flames and once again with great tenderness undressed each other and lay among cushions covered with the wolfskin coverlet.

Eden caressed Tom. She told him, 'There is something about your skin, the scent of it, its smoothness. I like touching you, it makes me feel very raunchy.'

Tom gazed into her eyes. A look passed between them then, something so intimate and exciting that words seemed superfluous. Silence seemed the order of things. Sexuality, all things erotic, a landscape of lust, passion, discovery, the outer limits of orgasm where oblivion and bliss ruled their lives, were waiting to be explored.

Eden moved on to her knees, yearning for the deepest penetration possible from Tom. He took her time and again with thrusts of hard pulsating cock and sweet kisses on her back. He licked her skin and sucked on her flesh and she felt as if he were branding her with hot metal, so extreme was the pleasure she derived from his fucking her.

Quite clearly he was a man used to adventurous sex and took enormous pleasure from coming with a woman. He was incredibly passionate, biting into Eden's flesh, reaching into her cunt with his fingers and scooping out the nectar of her orgasms. He licked them and offered her a taste, then returned to her with his phallus. He adored fucking Eden. They were made for sex together. He was enchanted by her lustful ways. It excited his imagination to hear heavy breathing, sounds of sexual joy. It was utter bliss to him to drive on and pleasure her in any way possible.

Tom reached into a lacquered box of beautiful carved sex toys. He knew from pure instinct that Eden was sexually mature and lustful enough to have used them before in erotic game-playing. He knew very well how to excite a woman with them and when she called out with enormous pleasure from one orgasm to another he knew they would always be able to enjoy the outer limits of sexual bliss together. They were a couple tuned into the joys of sexual freedom, no-holds-barred erotic nirvana.

Dawn turned into morning and they were still playing for high stakes sex where passion was king and love was god. Eden was lost in ecstasy.

A bright future seemed to hang in the air around them. It was warm and secure and both were aware how lucky they had been to come along in each other's life at that moment. The Max machine of public relations for the Epidaurus concerts was now in full swing, and Tom had coped with that admirably. He appreciated Eden's celebrity as if it was his own, modestly, and with wonder that such a rare and beautiful artist as she was to be his wife.

It was Tom who suggested that their marriage should not overshadow her comeback concerts, and there was no getting around it, they were two famous people whose wedding would be headline news. As the weeks went by they yearned to be husband and wife. While having a wedding certificate had never been an issue to either of them before, suddenly it became very important.

One fine day, after listening for several hours to Eden's rendition of Schubert, moved by the music and profoundly touched by her playing, Tom said, 'I don't want us to fool around any longer, I want to be married. We can keep it a secret until after the concerts but let's not wait. I'll pull all the right strings and cut through the red tape. So let's do it, get married in Hydra. What do you think?'

'What a good idea,' Eden told him, her heart racing

with anticipation. The very idea of being married to Tom brought tears of joy to her eyes.

Four days later all the arrangements were made. They stayed in Eden's house in Hydra. The church was closed to the public and Eden, wearing a cream-coloured dress by Yves St Laurent and white stephanotis pinned in her hair, and Tom, in blazer and old school tie, were married there amongst hundreds of white candles. An archbishop and two priests conducted the Greek Orthodox cere-mony. Max gave the bride away while Tom's friend Jason Wildeman was a witness.

The smell of burning wax mixed with incense. When the crowns were passed over the couple's heads the bride wept with a new kind of joy and thought of her mother, and how she would have adored every moment of Eden and Tom's wedding.

They slipped quietly out of the side door of the church and rushed home to her house after the ceremony. They saw no one for several days, but cooked and made love and Eden played marvellous music for her husband. She and the Surabaya were now attuned to each other, knew how to get the best from each other. Eden and Tom flew back England when their marriage had been duly celebrated, and lived and loved as they had before.

Chapter 18

Tom rarely spoke to Eden about his years covering the news. She gained the information more through his photographs as he assembled the book he was contracted to deliver, discovering searing displays of man's inhumanity to man. She soon realised that though her husband was able detach himself from the emotional trauma of such sights as he had seen, he had done so from pure survival instinct or he would never have been able to stomach the job, be the photographer he was.

How much he'd suffered was made clear to Eden only in the night when he slept restlessly, broke out in a sweat of terror, or called out and wept. At those times she would wake him from his nightmares as quietly and calmly as possible so that he might sleep once more a dreamless sleep. They never talked about the horrors that disturbed him. Eden somehow knew he would one day find the right moment to share his distress and bring it out into the light. Until then it was enough that she knew he needed her, and he knew she would be there for him.

As the concerts drew closer Eden often thought about that time when she had allowed herself to become an invisible woman. She had never before realised how strong and courageous a person she was. How at the moment of the death of herself she would be able to fight against it. That Tom should have been the catalyst to drive her back into life and then become a part of that life was still a miracle to her and one she would never take for granted.

Eden's happiness seemed boundless. She was grateful for every good thing happening to her but sometimes felt concern that it might not last, that something dark and evil would look upon her and say, 'Enough! You've had your share of greatness, of love. Why should it be you and not me?'

At moments like that Eden would remind herself that she was a positive, vibrant human being who had fallen into the pit of fear once and that was enough. She had lost herself, and found her way back. She would never let that happen to her again.

Two weeks before the concerts at Epidaurus approaches were made to Tom to photograph Saddam Hussein. The assignment was supposedly hush-hush, the interview to be conducted by Jason Wildeman. He was calling in a favour which put Tom on the spot. He did not see how he could refuse. The great portrait photographer Karsh would never have refused such a commission was all Eden had to say about the matter. Tom had covered the Gulf War and had been praised for his work by Hussein himself. He had no desire to be involved in anything in Iraq again, only to remain with Eden.

But it was a huge opportunity and eventually Eden herself suggested that he should go to Iraq and they would meet up several days before the concert. The house in Hydra was chosen as the rendezvous. Max would take care of everything. And so they parted for the first time since they had come together. Tom looked profoundly sad. Eden found it not so much sad as curious that he was not at her side. She made light of the matter, claiming she had much to do before the concert. They agreed not to speak every day since communication was never easy when Tom was out in the field.

For the first few days they did, however, speak to each other in spite of declaring they would not be dependent on phone calls. Then the calls stopped. Eden was not unduly concerned. She worked feverishly and was as critical as ever of her own performance. It was all going well, just as she expected it to. The usual anxieties over her interpretation, the excitement of returning to playing in public after so long a silence. It was all there, it was all happening.

Only at night alone in her bed while she was feeling a need for sexual fulfilment did she yearn for Tom. The nights reminded her of how glorious sex was with the man one loves. She thought about how powerful a sexual drive they both had and how wondrous it was to be on the edge of desire all the time. There had been only one other person in her life who could match that excitement and that had been Garfield. She would not deny that, she just let it be.

There was always a fuss before a concert and the house was a busy, bustling place. Eden's dresser always took too many clothes and shoes, always too many shoes. And there was always the make-up man and hairdresser on hand too making some sort of fuss. Eden took it all in her stride. Max listened to Laurent about the problems he'd had with his timetable removing all of that from Eden's shoulders.

She was calm and playing like an angel. She was cool, without any anxiety about Tom. She knew he would not fail her. He would be there days before she played. It was Eden's habit to move into a hotel before a performance. Max arranged that she should have her usual suite of rooms at Claridge's. She dined in the hotel restaurant or in her rooms, removed from the mundane demands of life. Tom knew where she would be if he was able to get in touch with her.

The days passed by pleasantly and with a great many interviews and photo shoots. The Surabaya was of special interest. Everyone wanted to know the history of the Stradivarius. Until recently Eden had rarely told the romantic story of the later years of the cello. Then a reporter from the *Times* asked her, 'There is so much mystery surrounding the Surabaya, why are you so reluctant to talk about it?'

Eden answered, 'Until it was given to me, I felt I had no right to talk about it. There is no real mystery, though. It holds no secrets. It has been through a great deal, survived two world wars. Because of it a family survived the holocaust. A Nazi SS man ran a house to house search for it and out of frustration murdered innocent people because the instrument eluded him. All that is history and well documented.

'There's romance in its story too because a German Jew called Albrecht Stein, a maker of fine pianos, one of those who thought of himself first as a German and second as a Jew, believed in his country and that Nazism could not survive and waited too late to leave Germany. By the time he was allowed to leave it was with nothing but the Stradivarius, and only then because he bribed his way out.

'The Stein family pooled all their money to buy the cello. They were a cultured lot and knew their investment was safe if they could get it to the West. At that time Japan had not bombed Pearl Harbour. The only passage the Stein family could get was to Malaysia where a cousin ran a rubber plantation and would take them in. The cello was taken as collateral against loans and so it remained for years in a cupboard in Surabaya. The Malaysian banker had a young wife who wanted to play the instrument. She had a passion for its sound and he could deny her nothing. Until Japan bombed Pearl Harbour and the Japanese occupied Malaysia, Mr Stein taught her the cello. They always referred to it as the Surabaya. It was hidden by the Malay banker until the end of the war when it was brought to the West and sold here.'

'What happened to the Stein family?'

'Tragically they all died in internment camps or working as forced labour in Japan.'

'And the young wife?' asked another reporter.

'She was a fine cellist until her death only a few years ago.'

'The Malay banker?'

'The money for which he sold the Surabaya helped to put the country's economy back on track after the war.'

'And now it's yours,' commented a young female reporter from a glossy magazine.

'Yes, now it's mine,' answered Eden and stood up to leave the room.

She was dining alone in the restaurant that evening. Max was dealing with final arrangements. Eden had become thoughtful, having told the story of the Surabaya, and wanted not to be alone but to have the buzz of people around her. However, she was quite shocked to find someone she knew standing over her. It took her several seconds to get herself under control.

It was Dante. Of course, he would know her pattern. Where she would be, when she would be there. Hadn't he seen it enough when she had been with Garfield?

'Go away, Dante,' she told him.

'Please, I know how much you dislike me but hear me out. I have come on behalf of Garfield. He's desperate, he needs you. He is still hopelessly in love with you. Just five minutes of your time. Please let me sit down and talk to you?'

The pain that Dante had caused Eden! It was as sharp in her memory as ever it had been. She wanted never to speak to him again but she also hated to have a scene in the restaurant that might be picked up by the news media. She was certain that if she did not give him some time he would indeed cause a scene. Dante was a brilliant drama queen. That was mostly the way he got everything he wanted.

'Five minutes then, Dante. Not a minute more.' And she indicated that he could take a chair.

The hovering waiters held one out for Dante and asked politely if he was dining with Miss Sidd.

'No,' she quickly answered for him.

'I will have only coffee and see the dessert trolley,' announced Dante.

So typical of him. Give him an inch and he took a mile. 'Was that necessary, Dante? I don't believe you will be served and have eaten your dessert and talked to me about Garfield in just five minutes.'

'You've become hard, Eden. I think I liked you better when you were in love with Garfield. So soft and malleable.'

'Time is ticking by, Dante,' she told him as she pushed away her plate. She had lost her appetite.

The dessert trolley arrived at the table. A place was set for Dante. He took his time in choosing one of the delectable confections, the waiters poured the coffee and Dante flirted with the young boys. Then quite suddenly they were gone and he and Eden were alone.

'I estimate that you have one minute left to say what

you have to say. So get on with it, Dante.'

'I made a mistake tearing you away from Garfield. For that I am sorry. I confess, I was jealous of the love he had for you. You simply did not understand the bond there is between Garfield and myself and you excluded me from your life with him, a grave mistake on your part. But we won't go into all that. Garfield is in love with you, he wants back what you once had together. I am here pleading his case because I am sure that this time round we can all reach a better understanding.

'You are still in love with him! No one falls out of a love as strong as the one you had for each other. Admit it, you still love Garfield. If you could have that love back again you would grab it with both hands.' The unctuous smile on Dante's lips as he spoke the truths that Eden did not want to hear seared into her heart.

'Why didn't he come himself, so we could at last resolve this great love he walked out on?' she asked.

Eden noted Dante's smug expression. She rose from her chair, suggesting, 'If all that you said is true, then tell him he must come and plead his own case. He will find me in Hydra in two days' time.' Then without another word she walked away from her table and her unwelcome guest.

Eden could not get Garfield out of her mind. It had been the most exciting, the deepest, love she had ever had. She had succumbed to a gigolo's charm and fallen in love with Garfield, the love affair of a lifetime. She wanted to be thinking of Tom but Garfield's was a stronger presence and she knew she had to be with him one more time or wonder for the remainder of her life.

Where was Tom? She followed her schedule. Hopefully he would be in Hydra by the time she arrived there.

But he was not.

In Athens, through the Peloponnese, on the islands of Hydra, Spetses, Poros, every bed was reserved for the return of Eden Sidd playing at Epidaurus. It was the musical sensation of the decade. Max had promoted it with such style, all the music-loving world wanted to be there. It did wonders for Greece. That she had chosen Epidaurus from everywhere else available to her was certainly a coup for the country.

In a party of three Eden and two of Max's assistants flew from London to Athens where Max met Eden and her two cellos. She had never let them out of her sight. There was a photo-shoot as she boarded the helicopter that would take her to Hydra. She smiled, she cooed at the press and realised that she had been wrong to have given up playing in public. This reception quite overwhelmed her. In truth, as she had forgotten herself, she had come to believe her admirers had too. Eden felt quite humble now, knowing she would never again disappoint her public.

The helicopter landed high up on Hydra, away from the port, which was unusual but arranged so that Eden could walk down to her house and not have to face the islanders who would be overwhelmingly hospitable and want an immediate celebration.

Her first question should have been, 'Has Tom

arrived?' It was not, some instinct telling her he hadn't but that it didn't matter. He would be there when he would be there. She walked down the hill to her house, her cellos balanced on either side of a donkey.

When she entered the courtyard of her house she could hear voices, a man's voice speaking very bad Greek and a woman's, her housekeeper. Her heart skipped several beats and then she saw him, Garfield, looking more handsome than ever. She felt a rush of excitement. He saw her and abandoned the housekeeper to walk towards Eden. He touched her hair with his fingers, kissed her cheek, oozing that special sensuality that she was incapable of ignoring. Max entered the courtyard behind her and was instantly aghast at finding Garfield there.

Before he could utter a word Eden said, 'Max, I am very tired, I will see you in the morning unless it is something urgent?'

He was thrown by the presence of Garfield. The tone of Eden's voice, the look in her eyes, he well knew what they meant. She could not resist Garfield. The man was the devil incarnate. He had eaten into her soul, her will dissolved before his. Max left them together and could only think what bad luck it was that Tom was not there.

Eden wanted Garfield. She had always wanted Garfield. He had something sexual that she found irresistible. She could come by the mere touch of his hand upon her breast; a gentle kiss from him could make her weep with emotion. He had a smug expression on his face. She could imagine him saying to himself,

'I've got you! You'll come with me without my even having to touch you. But I will because I know that's what you want.' She felt the warmth that accompanies orgasm, the passion that knows no bounds. It felt delicious and exciting. And then she was reminded of his weakness and selfishness, the evil manipulation he was capable of, and all her sensual feelings for him died one more time and forever.

'If it's true that you love me, which is what Dante says, then get out of my house and my life, Garfield. There is no room in it for the likes of you. Make no mistake, for me you are the dark side of the moon. And there is no life, nothing can thrive and blossom on the dark side of the moon.'

'You bitch!'

Eden laughed and told him, 'I had a great teacher.' She held the door to the courtyard open and he walked out and never looked back.

Now there was only one day left before the concert and Tom had still not appeared. Max was aware that Garfield had not won Eden over and thanked God for it. But where was her husband?

During siesta there was a banging at the courtyard gate. Eden knew at once Tom had come home in time for the concert. She rushed to the gate and swung it open to fall into his arms.

They made love all through the night. Then it was here, the day had arrived. Eden, Tom, Max and the two cellos boarded a fast motor launch to cross to the Peloponnese where they were met by two cars and driven to Epidaurus. They went into a final morning rehearsal, Laurent, the orchestra and Eden in top form.

That night Eden was carefully dressed, her hair and make-up done, and right on schedule she stepped on to the stage at Epidaurus wearing a semi-transparent long dress of flesh-coloured silk organza that clung to her like a second skin. She looked all body and soul as, taking the Surabaya in her arms, she played it with godliness. Afterwards there was a fifteen-minute standing ovation that resounded through ancient Epidaurus. It was so dramatic, a night never to be forgotten. When Eden was asked to say a few words, she told her audience, 'It is with grateful thanks to you all that I appear tonight but most especially I would like to dedicate this concert to the memory of Albrecht Stein and his family who saved the Surabaya.'

Forbidden

Roberta Latow

Amy Ross, a celebrated art historian, has had many lovers in her lifetime. Again and again she has tasted the sweet ecstasy of sexual fulfilment and erotic depravity. Now, in her later years, she lives as a recluse, blissfully content in her own isolation, an enigma to her friends and admirers.

But Amy has suppressed the memory of her one secret obsession – her love affair with the artist Jarret Sparrow. Their relationship was beyond belief, her love for him dominated her entire life and took her to the furthest limits of carnal desire. Their feelings were too powerful to control – but their love for each other was ultimately forbidden.

Since their separation, Jarret and his manipulative Turkish friend Fee have seduced numerous women in pursuit of their ambition to conquer the art world. And now Jarret is about to re-enter Amy's life. For all those years, Amy had thought it was over. But is she prepared to rekindle the flames of her desire, and at what price . . . ?

'A wonderful storyteller. Her descriptive style is second to none . . . astonishing sexual encounters . . . exotic places, so real you can almost feel the hot sun on your back . . . heroines we all wish we could be' *Daily Express*

'Latow's writing is vibrant and vital. Her descriptions emanate a confidence and boldness that is typical of her characters' *Books* magazine

'It sets a hell of a standard' *The Sunday Times*

'Explicitly erotic . . . intelligently written' *Today*

0 7472 4911 3

HEADLINE

Objects of Desire

Roberta Latow

Suppressed passions, secret cravings and erotic fulfilment come together in this sensational novel of desire

Married to a world-famous surgeon, and mother of twin boys, Anoushka Rivers seems to lead a perfect life. But her erotic nature is suppressed by a man who does not love her.

Page Cooper has spent a decade longing for a man she can never have. For three weeks of each year, they experience the sweet ecstasy of desire, knowing that it cannot last.

Sally Brown is a good-time girl looking for love. When she finds it in the arms of Jahangir, a darkly sensuous Indian prince, her sensuality is awakened as never before.

Drawn together, these dynamic women explore their true potential – mentally, physically and sexually. A liaison with a seductive stranger on board the QE2; an afternoon of erotic depravity in Paris; a lustful *ménage à trois* overlooking the Taj Mahal; endless nights and days of unbridled passion with men willing to submit to their every desire, exploring fantasies beyond belief. In their search for new horizons, they find within themselves a strength and peace of mind more satisfying than anything else. These women are truly – Objects of Desire.

0 7472 4866 4

HEADLINE

Her Hungry Heart

Roberta Latow

He was handsome, tall and slender, with bedroom
eyes that devoured women. She was a tall willowy
blonde with the looks of a showgirl, wealthy, cultivated and intelligent, an enchantress who knew how
to tame men and, once they were tamed, clever
enough to keep them. They met on New Year's Eve
1943 at a chic party in New York's fashionable
Stork Club. Their erotic attraction was immediate
and mutual. Their love affair would last a lifetime.
But Karel Stefanik was not free to love Barbara
Dunmellyn. He had Mimi, whom he had abandoned
in the cruel chaos of war, a child whose fate becomes
inextricably entangled with that of her father and the
woman he loves.

This, then, is the story of their hungry hearts, the
lovers that fuel their lives; and finally of their own all-
encompassing love.

'The first lady of hanky panky. Her books are solidly
about sex . . . it adds a frisson. It sets a hell of a
standard' *The Sunday Times*

'Naughty, certainly . . . the sex is larded with dollops
of exoticism and luxury' *Observer*

'A sunshine sizzler, packed with non-stop sex'
People magazine

0 7472 3884 7

HEADLINE

Now you can buy any of these other bestselling
Headline books from your bookshop or
direct from the publisher.

FREE P&P AND UK DELIVERY
(Overseas and Ireland £3.50 per book)

Olivia's Luck	Catherine Alliott	£5.99
Backpack	Emily Barr	£5.99
Girlfriend 44	Mark Barrowcliffe	£5.99
Seven-Week Itch	Victoria Corby	£5.99
Two Kinds of Wonderful	Isla Dewar	£6.99
Fly-Fishing	Sarah Harvey	£5.99
Bad Heir Day	Wendy Holden	£5.99
Good at Games	Jill Mansell	£5.99
Sisteria	Sue Margolis	£5.99
For Better, For Worse	Carole Matthews	£5.99
Something For the Weekend		
	Pauline McLynn	£5.99
Far From Over	Sheila O'Flanagan	£5.99

TO ORDER SIMPLY CALL THIS NUMBER

01235 400 414

or e-mail <u>orders@bookpoint.co.uk</u>

Prices and availability subject to change without notice.